To Peter ~

I hope you enjoy

" Finding 1492 "

Best wishes !

Finding 1492

by

BRIAN CANNICI

authorHOUSE®

AuthorHouse™
1663 Liberty Drive, Suite 200
Bloomington, IN 47403
www.authorhouse.com
Phone: 1-800-839-8640

First published by AuthorHouse 4/7/2008

ISBN: 978-1-4343-5294-1 (sc)

Library of Congress Control Number: 2008901923

Printed in the United States of America
Bloomington, Indiana

This book is printed on acid-free paper.

For my wife, Cindy, and
our beautiful children, Nicholas and Julianna

"Every one of us has in him a continent of undiscovered character. Blessed is he who acts the Columbus to his own soul."

~ Author Unknown

Part 1

Finders Keepers

Chapter 1

IT WAS A PICTURESQUE SATURDAY afternoon in Monroe Park. The mid-June weather that marked the coming of summer made for a perfect day to play a ball game, and what a game it was! The two best teams in the Monroe Park Little League were locked in a contest that was turning out to be one for the ages! The Blue Knights were holding onto a one-run lead against the unbeaten Wildcats in the bottom of the final inning. There was one out, runners at first and third, and you could cut the tension with a knife as the next hitter came to the plate for the Cats.

Brandon Morelli and Shawn Thompson looked at each other from their positions in the middle infield. They knew that their pitcher (who had hurled the game of his life) was tiring, and their chances of putting a blemish on the opposing team's unbeaten record was hanging by a thread. The momentum of the game was certainly not in their favor right now, especially since one of the Wildcats' best hitters was coming to the plate. Tension was high and nerves were firing on all cylinders. Normally the last thing in the world a kid wanted in this situation was for the ball to be hit to him. But these two boys were cut from a different mold. They actually *wanted* the ball!

Brandon and Shawn were best friends, and they happened to make up the best middle-infield tandem in the league: Brandon at shortstop, Shawn at second base. Both had great hands, swift feet, strong arms, and a knack for putting themselves in just the right position, depending on the hitter. These were rare qualities for boys their age.

"Let's see if we can get two here," Brandon said confidently to his partner. "Okay. Let's do this," replied Shawn.

The runners prepared to take their leads as the Knights' pitcher began his windup toward the plate. The delivery came swiftly.

"Ball!" the umpire yelled after his first pitch sailed too high.

A muffled groan could be heard from the crowd of Knights' fans who watched nervously. The Wildcats' slugger looked confidently to his bench and smiled after getting ahead in the count with the first pitch. As his pitcher received the ball back from the catcher, Brandon pounded his fist into his glove and shouted words of encouragement.

"Come on now! You can do it! No free passes here!"

The exhausted hurler took a very deep breath as he looked in for his sign and then checked the runners. With focus and determination, he locked into his catcher's target once more and fired the ball. The pitch came right down the middle, not where you wanted to throw the ball against a good hitter like this. The wide-eyed, teeth-clenching slugger ripped the ball high and deep down the third-base line. Going! Going! Back! Back! _FOUL!_ The would-be winning shot missed the inside of the foul pole by three feet. Whew! That was close. The hitter jogged back to the batter's box and picked up his bat. Confidence was just _oozing_ out of him. Another mistake like that from the pitcher, and he knew he wouldn't miss again.

The count was one ball, one strike. Once again the pitcher took a deep breath, checked the runners, and looked in for the sign. With a loud grunt, he proceeded to throw a fastball that was destined to hit its target for a strike. In the next second, a sound came from the hitter's aluminum bat that seemed like the loudest sound Shawn had ever heard. Ping! The ball was hit on the ground hard, and it was headed up the middle for what many in the bleachers thought was the winning hit. That's when Shawn did the unthinkable. He dove to his right, stretching as far as his eleven-year-old body could go. Amazingly the ball found its way into his glove, and without hesitation, Shawn flipped it to Brandon, who by instinct, was waiting on the bag to turn the double play. The execution was flawless. The catch. The transfer from glove to hand. The pivot. The deadly accurate throw to first. Double play! Game over! Knights win!

The next day was the last day of school before summer vacation. Brandon and Shawn had enjoyed all of the attention and hero treatment they had received during the week after the big win against the Wildcats. However, the boys were ready for summer, and like most kids their age, they couldn't wait for school to be over.

Before the students in Thomas Edison Elementary School could celebrate the final moments of their fifth-grade experience, report cards had to be distributed. For some of them, this was a moment of anxiety, but not for the two new heroes. The boys were very good students. Any anxiety they felt was focused on whether or not they would be in the same homeroom next year. They had always been in the same class, and to be separated was a possibility they couldn't even imagine.

One by one, the students were handed their report cards in alphabetical order. Brandon received his before Shawn, since the "M" in his last name came before "T," but he didn't open it. He waited until his best pal got his. The two walked toward each other nervously with the report cards still folded neatly inside their envelopes.

"On three," Shawn said. "One. Two. Three!"

The two of them quickly pulled out the report cards, paying no attention to their grades. Their eyes shifted directly to the bottom right of the card where the words *Assignment for Next Year* were typed. In the space next to these words, both boys read out loud, *Class 6-B!* A wild celebration ensued.

"Yeah!" yelled Shawn.

"You can't break up the Dream Team!" exclaimed Brandon.

After they quickly scanned their final grades, the next order of business was to see who they would have next year for social studies, one of their favorite subjects. They knew from their friends in the grades above that Mr. Coviello was the man you wanted. "Mr. C," as he was affectionately known, was a young, energetic teacher who had a reputation for making his classes really fun and interesting. It was also said that Mr. C happened to be a _huge_ sports nut, who particularly loved baseball. This promised to be a perfect match for the boys, but would the good luck they enjoyed so far continue? They looked over the copies of the new sixth-grade schedules that listed their classes and their assigned teachers. Quickly and carefully they both came upon their destination:

Social Studies 6B – Mr. Coviello

Their streak of good luck lived on! They were going to be in the same homeroom _and_ they were going to have the best social studies teacher in Eisenhower Middle School. Sixth grade was already off to a great start, and they hadn't even been dismissed from fifth grade yet! The boys couldn't be any happier. When the final bell rang, Brandon and Shawn gave cheers of celebration with their friends, and then headed for the outdoor basketball courts to hang out and shoot some hoops. It would probably be the last time they would be together with all of their fifth-grade friends like this. Summer vacations, a new school, and new friends were all on the horizon, but the kids didn't give much thought to that. Whether it was the innocence of their age or something else, it didn't matter. They enjoyed the present moments for what they were.

Eventually all of the kids tired and made their way home, bringing an official end to their time at Thomas Edison Elementary School.

Chapter 2

SUMMER VACATION HAD FINALLY ARRIVED! School was over. No homework or studying for two whole months. Life was good. Brandon and Shawn had made plans for the entire break. No day would be wasted. There would be Wiffle ball games, swimming at the town pool, overnight camping trips (in each other's backyards), barbeques, movies, and of course, baseball. There would, however, be an additional activity added to this list that would come as a complete surprise to the boys. It happened one morning when Brandon's parents called him to the table.

Mr. and Mrs. Morelli waited for their only child to come down the stairs. When he entered the kitchen, Brandon could tell from the looks on their faces that something was up. Mr. Morelli spoke first.

"Son, before you eat your breakfast, your mother and I would like to share some news with you."

"O-kaaaay," Brandon said slowly and carefully.

"Well it's been a while since we took a vacation together as a family. Your mother and I have been busy with work, and you've been busy with school and baseball. It's just been hard to find time. Anyway, we think it's time for us to get away, and August appears to be the perfect month to do it. Mom and I both put in for some time off then, and your baseball season will be finished at that point."

"Cool," said Brandon. "So where are we going?"

Mrs. Morelli was the one who revealed their destination.

"Punta Cana!" she said excitedly.

"Punta *who*???"

"Punta Cana. It's a region in the Dominican Republic. We're going to stay at a vacation resort there for a week! Isn't that wonderful?"

"Yeah. That does sound pretty cool. What kinda things can we do down there?"

"Oh there's plenty to do. We have a lot of time to talk about that," said Mr. Morelli. "But there's one more surprise we have for you."

"Really? What is it?" Brandon's excitement really began to grow.

"We took the liberty of calling Mrs. Thompson and asked her if it was okay if Shawn came with us ... she said *yes*!"

"Shawn's coming??? Yes! This is going to be the coolest trip ever! Thank you!"

The Morellis embraced in a group hug. Brandon's face was all smiles.

The month of July seemed to go by quickly, and the last weeks were filled with excitement and anticipation. The boys couldn't wait to hit Punta Cana. From what Mr. Morelli had told them, there was an array of activities for them there. They had catamaran boat rides, parasailing, sports fishing, snorkeling, glass bottom boats for marine life observation, and all kinds of tours. The possibilities were endless.

"What do you think we'll do first?" asked Shawn. "Man, I want to get one of those Dominican Republic jerseys from the World Baseball Classic. They almost won the whole thing you know."

"I know" said Brandon. "I can't believe *Japan* won. Anyway, we probably won't have a lot of time for souvenir shopping with all of the stuff there is to do down there. Hey, you know Jenna Estevez?"

"Yeah."

"Well she went snorkeling with her family over the summer last year, and she said it was one of the coolest things she ever did. I *definitely* want to try that."

"Okay. Sounds good to me. Hey wait a minute. Are there any sharks in the water down there? I don't want to become lunch for a giant fish you know. That's not the way for a proud young black man to go out."

"What are you worried about? The thing would probably spit you out!"

On hearing the tongue-in-cheek insult from his friend, Shawn pranced into his best Muhammad Ali fighting stance and began to shadow box. Not to be outdone, Brandon threw *his* hands up and moved his way toward his sparring partner, doing his best Rocky Marciano impression. It was the boxer vs. the bruiser. Both boys moved around faking jabs, hooks, overhand rights, and uppercuts. Whenever they got into this, the sparring usually lasted about five minutes. No real punches were ever thrown of course. It was just a whole lot of footwork and movement, a contest to see who looked more like a real boxer. Each participant always claimed victory for himself.

"Oh man, I would have knocked you out with that one!"

"Yeah right. Saw it coming a mile away. You couldn't touch me."

On and on it went until both boys dropped from exhaustion.

"Hey man, I gotta go. Still got a lot of packing to do," said Shawn.

"All right. I still have some stuff to do too," shared Brandon.

"I'll see you later."

"Later."

Both boys went home very tired but still full of excitement. They would be leaving for Punta Cana in three days.

Chapter 3

ON THE MORNING OF DEPARTURE, Shawn awoke to a knock on his bedroom door. It was his mother. She looked like she woke up very early.

"You all packed and ready to go baby?" she asked.

"Huh? Oh yeah," a groggy Shawn replied.

"Let's see now, I packed your clothes, your bathing suit, your toothbrush, a camera to take pictures, your —"

"Didn't we do this last night Mama?" He rubbed his eyes until they came into focus.

"Yes, but it's always good to double-check. Now Mr. Morelli has the plane tickets and your passport. You stay close to him and mind what he tells you. There are a lot of crazy people out there, and I don't need my baby —"

"I'll be *fine* Mama," Shawn interrupted. "Don't worry. I'll take lots of pictures, and if you're good, I might bring you something back."

The two of them laughed and embraced. They had always been close, and Mrs. Thompson had always been very protective of her son. It took some convincing on Mr. Morelli's part when he asked her if Shawn could go on the trip. She eventually agreed because she knew how close the two boys were, and she trusted the Morellis. They had always treated her son as if he were a part of their family.

Although the trip would mark the first time they would be apart for an extended period, Mrs. Thompson knew that it was time to let Shawn spread his wings. He wasn't a little boy anymore, and a vacation in the Dominican Republic was something that she would not deny him.

At 9 a.m. sharp, Shawn and his mother heard the Morelli's car horn in their driveway. It was time to go. Mrs. Thompson gave Shawn one more giant hug, and kissed his head before opening the front door. When she did, she was greeted by Brandon and his parents. Mr. Morelli was dressed in a festive Hawaiian shirt, shorts, and a straw fedora hat. When he saw Mrs. Thompson standing in her doorway, he spread out his arms, looked at himself, and asked, "What do you think?"

The answer to his question came in the form of a hearty laugh.

"Oh Lord," Mrs. Thompson said after she caught her breath.

The boys began to load Shawn's bags into the car with the help of Mr. Morelli. While they did, the ladies chatted.

"Thank you again for taking Shawn. You have no idea how excited he is about this trip."

"Oh I'm sure I have a pretty good idea," said Mrs. Morelli. "And it's our pleasure."

"You'll call me as soon as you land?"

"Of course, as soon as we land. I think the boys are really going to enjoy this. Bob and I went to Punta Cana on our honeymoon, and it's just beautiful."

Once the car was packed, everyone said their good-byes to Mrs. Thompson. As the car pulled out of the driveway, Shawn blew a kiss to his mother and smiled as if to say "Don't worry." They were on their way to the airport. The Dominican Republic was just hours away.

Chapter 4

THEIR FLIGHT LANDED IN PUNTA Cana International Airport at around 1:30 p.m. Eastern time. It was a fairly smooth flight with bad food and a good movie. After retrieving their luggage from the claim area, they quickly walked through the airport. Brandon and Shawn were still discussing the highlights of their first trip on an airplane. It was an amazing experience for both of them. As promised, Mrs. Morelli called Shawn's mother to let her know they landed and were okay.

A shuttle van from the Casa de Coral Hotel and Resort waited for them in front of the airport, a welcome sight for tired feet and heavy hands. Mr. Morelli introduced himself to the driver and informed him that they were guests at the hotel, showing him the necessary paperwork. The driver, a very friendly gentleman, warmly greeted them.

"Welcome to Punta Cana my friends," he said with an accent that was unmistakably Dominican. "My name is

Manny. Please have a seat in the van and make yourselves comfortable. We'll be leaving for the hotel shortly."

Carefully he began to load their luggage into the van. Three minutes later, they were on their way.

Everyone was relieved to be seated and rested in the van. Walking through the airport with all of their luggage had been very tiring. As the van moved, the boys took in the sights, observing the people and counting the coconut palms as they passed.

"So where in America are you from amigos?" asked Manny.

"How did you know we're from America?" Mr. Morelli responded. He knew it was a foolish response, being that they probably stuck out like sore thumbs. This thought was verified by Manny, who laughed as if hearing a funny joke.

"Just a wild guess my friend. Is this your first time in our country?"

"Actually no. My wife and I honeymooned here. However, it *is* the first time for the boys."

"Ah. Young amigos, I think you are going to love it here. Plenty for you to do to have fun. The resort area has beautiful beaches and very friendly people. Sadly, things are not always so nice outside the resorts. The Dominican Republic is a very poor country, and travelers can find trouble if they are in the wrong places. Everything you need is in the resort area. Please do not leave it."

"Oh don't worry," Mr. Morelli said. "We've already been through this with them, but I'm glad that they are hearing it from someone who lives here. Thank you."

"No problema. We want our visitors here to be safe and happy."

A few minutes later, the van pulled up to the front of the hotel.

"Well here we are," Manny said. "The beautiful Casa de Coral Hotel. Let me get your bags for you."

Manny made his way to the back of the van and unloaded the luggage. When he was done, a bellhop from the hotel arrived almost on cue, and began to stack the luggage on a cart. They could tell right away that this was a first-class operation.

"Good-bye my friends. Enjoy your stay in our country."

"Thank you Manny," Mr. Morelli said. "It was very nice meeting you."

Mr. Morelli had something folded up in his hand as he extended it to Manny. Brandon saw that it was money, and knew that his father was giving him a tip. "You have to take care of the people who take care of you," his father always told him. "It's important."

"Thank you very much sir. Enjoy!"

Manny waved, got back into the van, and drove away. They followed the bellhop into the hotel and prepared to check in.

The lobby of the Casa de Coral was really impressive. With wide eyes and open mouths, Brandon and Shawn took in the tropical scenery while they waited for their room keys. They had never seen anything like it. When they finally got to their rooms, they threw their bags on the beds and ran straight for the balcony. The view was unbelievable. They saw the tremendous hotel pool. It was huge! Beyond that, they could see the white sands of the beach, the ocean, and the many beautiful palm trees that surrounded the area.

"So what do you think gentleman?" asked Mr. Morelli. "Nice place?"

"Uh-huh," Brandon said incredulously.

"What do you say we quickly get unpacked, get something to eat, and check everything out?" Mrs. Morelli suggested.

"Sounds like a plan to me," said Shawn.

After everyone unpacked their things, they went to a restaurant near the hotel. They were seated at an outdoor table, which offered a beautiful view of their tropical environment. After lunch was ordered, the main topic of discussion was which activity they would explore first. Several ideas were thrown around, and then Brandon spoke up.

"Mom and Dad, Shawn and I were talking about what we wanted to do first before we even came here. We heard from one of our friends at school that snorkeling is really cool. Would it be okay if we tried that first?"

"Well I don't see why not," said Mr. Morelli. "I'll tell you what, we'll make that our main activity for tomorrow, since it will be our first full day here. Sound good?"

"Yeah!" the boys shouted enthusiastically.

Brandon and Shawn gave each other a high-five, and pumped their fists with excitement. Mr. and Mrs. Morelli looked at each other and laughed. Tomorrow they were going snorkeling. They didn't know it yet, but this experience was going to change their lives in more ways than one.

Chapter 5

THE FIRST FULL DAY IN Punta Cana began with breakfast at a small restaurant in the hotel lobby. While everyone ate, Mr. Morelli outlined the plan for the day. He announced that he and the two boys would be headed to El Cortecito beach to go on their snorkeling excursion, while Mrs. Morelli planned to spend the better part of the day at Bavaro Plaza, the largest shopping area at the resort. Everyone was excited to begin their day, but no one more than Brandon. He had been thinking about it all night.

When they finished eating, they all waited in front of the hotel for their respective shuttle vans to pick them up. Mrs. Morelli's came first.

"Well I'm off. You boys have a great time and please be careful. The water can be so dangerous. I want to hear about everything when I get back, okay?"

"Sure honey. We'll be fine," her husband said reassuringly.

"Yeah Mom, don't worry," added Brandon. "This is going to be great!"

"Okay then. Have fun!" Mrs. Morelli said as she got into the van. Slowly it pulled away.

"Take care Mrs. Morelli!" said Shawn.

Ten minutes later, the shuttle van to El Cortecito beach arrived. Mr. Morelli joined the boys in exchanging high-fives as if they were preparing to play in a big game.

"Okay boys, here we go!"

They got in the van and talked about the adventure that awaited them.

Brandon's dad began to prepare them for what they needed to do once they reached their destination.

"Listen carefully boys. I asked someone at the information desk in the hotel what we needed to do today. He said that first we need to go to the equipment rental shop to get our gear. Then he recommended that we hook up with an instructor since none of us have ever done this before. Guys, I want you to listen and pay attention to what the instructor tells you. No fooling around, okay?"

"Okay Dad," said Brandon.

"No problem Mr. Morelli," said Shawn.

"Good. I think we're really going to have a great time."

The van pulled up right in front of the rental shop. They got off and headed inside. Brandon and Shawn walked around the shop while Mr. Morelli spoke to a woman behind the counter about getting equipment and instruction.

"I want a big oxygen tank and a harpoon gun, man," Shawn informed Brandon.

"A harpoon gun? We're going snorkeling Shawn. We're not going shark hunting!"

"Yeah I know. Be pretty cool if they let us have one though."

"I guess. You'd probably end up shooting our instructor in the foot with it."

The boys broke into laughter as they continued to look around. A few minutes later, Mr. Morelli called them up to the counter in front of the shop. He had a basket full of equipment with him. When the boys looked in the basket, they were surprised to see that there were no oxygen tanks, wet suits, or even harpoon guns in there. Instead they saw masks, snorkels, and three pairs of swim fins.

"That's it? That's all we need?" Brandon asked his father.

"Yeah that's it. What did you expect, a harpoon gun?" The boys quickly looked at each other and smirked.

"We have to walk outside to the back of the shop and wait for our instructor now. He will take us out to the water and get us started."

With their equipment in tow, they made their way to the back of the shop, which was located right on the beach. A short while later, a tall dark man approached them and introduced himself.

"Hello gentlemen. My name is David. I understand that you are interested in learning how to snorkel today."

"Very nice to meet you David." said Mr. Morelli. "This is my son, Brandon, and this is his best friend, Shawn."

"A pleasure to meet you boys. Welcome to El Cortecito beach. The first thing we are going to do today is get into a boat. We will be traveling to a spot near the reef where the water is very calm and warm. Once we are there, I will show you how to use your equipment and explain the rules. Ready to go?"

"Yeah!" the boys answered.

"Okay then. Let's have some fun."

They got onto a small white motorboat that was docked near the shop. David showed them where to sit and started the engine with a thunderous roar, which prompted Shawn to say "Cool!" As the boat began to make its way, the boys took notice of their environment. They had never seen beautiful blue water like this before. The white sands down below made the visibility very clear.

"Sure isn't like the beach we go to every summer," observed Brandon.

"Nope. These are some of the most beautiful waters you will ever see son," said Mr. Morelli.

"Look at that!" said Shawn, pointing to a small school of fish darting by.

They continued observing the beauty of the water and the scenes below the surface when suddenly the boat began to slow down. It looked like this was the spot where they would be snorkeling.

"Okay we're here!" yelled David.

When the boat came to a complete stop, he emerged from the front of the vessel. Taking a seat by Mr. Morelli and the boys, he began to explain to them exactly what snorkeling was, and why people enjoy it so much. Mr. Morelli, Brandon, and Shawn listened closely. He showed them how to wear and use the equipment that they had rented. His instructions were clear and easy to follow. It seemed fairly simple to all of them. Finally it was time to get into the water. This was the moment of truth.

David secured his mask and his snorkel and jumped into the water. He then invited the boys and Mr. Morelli to join him. The water was just as he had described it, very calm and very warm.

"Okay. Is everyone ready? It's time to try it for real. Just relax, breathe calmly, and enjoy the scenery. There are so many beautiful things to see!"

The adventure had begun. As Brandon allowed his face to break the surface of the water, he thought to himself that David was absolutely right. There *were* so many beautiful things to see. It was a world of vibrant color and movement. The coral reef he first encountered presented itself as a collection of lifeless colored rocks, but Brandon remembered from his science class that these were living creatures. That fascinated him. He was amazed as he saw multi-hued fish darting among the coral heads, seemingly having no fear of his presence. He took notice of the soft corals, sponges, and sea fans that fluttered in the currents. There were also various forms of seaweed and algae to observe. Looking deeper, he saw starfish, sea urchins, and several crustaceans plodding along the ocean floor. It was absolutely unbelievable! After a while, he came to the realization that he wasn't sure how long he had been floating on the surface of the water. He had lost all sense of time. So he decided he would come up and see how Shawn and his father were doing. When he did, he noticed that the two of them were still at it, hearing the breaths that came from their snorkels. He laughed to himself.

"Do you want to try free diving Brandon?" a voice asked from behind him. It was David.

"Okay. What do I do?"

"It's simple. Just take a deep breath and swim down a few feet to get a closer look at the reef and the sea creatures. You'll enjoy it. Just keep in mind that you can't breathe through the snorkel while you are underwater."

"All right David. Here it goes."

"Good luck my friend!"

Brandon took a very deep breath and began his free dive. Wow! If he thought his first look from the surface of the water was special, it was *nothing* compared to this. He was now up close and personal with this tropical world. As he stroked further down, he imagined himself as one of the colorful fish he had observed, swimming along, looking for food. He completely lost himself in the experience. After surfacing to take another deep breath, he decided that on this dive he would closely examine the coral reef. As he closely inspected it, he noticed all of the different forms of life that made a home in it. He was truly amazed. Brandon took a few more seconds to look around before he surfaced again, when suddenly something caught his eye. There was an unusual object that appeared to be lodged between the corals near the bottom of the reef. He wasn't sure what it was, so he dove deeper to get a closer look. It appeared to be the case of an old pocket watch that a previous traveler had lost years ago. Did the case have any value? Could he pry it free? Any attempt at doing so would have to be done quickly, since he needed to get air in his lungs soon. With a tight grip and a quick pull, Brandon was able to dislodge the old case from the corals. He was shocked. He thought for sure that the object would be impossible to budge. He held the case tightly in his hand as he headed for the surface. He couldn't wait to show Shawn and his father what he had found.

Shawn and Mr. Morelli had finished snorkeling a few minutes before Brandon came up. They gave him a round of applause when his head emerged from the water.

"You were down there for a long time Brandon. Don't you ever get tired?" asked Shawn.

"I didn't think I was down there that long," said Brandon. "Once I started free diving, I wanted to see everything up close. It was awesome!"

"It sure was. Shawn and I were watching you the whole time. You did great son."

"Thanks Dad. This is one of the coolest things I've ever done."

"Well gentlemen," David interrupted, "it looks like our time is up. We have to get back to the shop. All of you did very well today. It must be my fine teaching."

Mr. Morelli and the boys nodded in agreement and laughed as they got into the boat.

On the boat ride back to the shop, the three of them shared the experiences of their underwater adventures. It was at this time that Brandon decided to reveal his discovery to Shawn and his father.

"Hey guys, look what I found lodged in the corals while I was snorkeling."

"What is that thing?" asked Shawn.

"I think it's a case from an old watch," said Brandon. "I figured it might be worth something. Look, there's something engraved on the back of it."

"Here, let me see it," said Mr. Morelli.

Carefully, Brandon's father inspected the case. There certainly was something engraved on the back, but it was very hard to tell what it said. A large part of the engraving had faded, and part of it had been scratched off from the corals. From the remaining letters on the back of the case, only two words could be distinguished.

"My Fire," Mr. Morelli said. "I wonder what that means. It could be the name of a ship, or it could be something else, maybe something symbolic. Very hard to tell. Anyway, this thing looks very old and beat up Brandon. It looks like time and the ocean have had their way with it."

"Yeah. I don't think it will have much value," said Shawn. "Why couldn't you find some gold coins or a diamond or something?"

"I'll try harder next time," said Brandon.

The three tired adventurers returned to the shop, and a little while later, the van came and brought them back to the hotel. When he returned to his room, Brandon tucked the case that he found in his travel bag and forgot about it for the rest of the trip. As a matter of fact, he forgot about the old case for the rest of the summer.

Chapter 6

THE SUMMER DAYS PASSED QUICKLY, as they always do for children who wish they would never end. Before the boys knew it, they were back at school. Even though they longed for an extended vacation, Brandon and Shawn were still fairly excited about the new school year. It would certainly be a year of new beginnings. They would be starting a new grade, and they would be attending a new school.

Eisenhower Middle School presented itself as another world to the incoming sixth-grade students on the first day. It was new, it was different, and boy was it big! The new school dwarfed Thomas Edison Elementary. Everything seemed super-sized. The hallways were bigger. The classrooms were bigger. Even the teachers looked bigger! As the day began, the wide-eyed and anxious newcomers moved through the hallways checking their schedules and looking for their classrooms like mice in a maze. Several of them could be seen with looks of confusion and anguish on their faces as they tried to crack the combination code to their lockers. Teachers stood outside of their classrooms providing directions and instructions for those students who seemed completely lost. It didn't take very long for school to be back in full swing!

Brandon and Shawn walked through the hallways observing their new surroundings. As they walked, they were greeted by many familiar faces from the fifth grade. Seeing these faces seemed to take the nervous edge off a little. Having already solved the mysteries of their schedules and their lockers, the boys were all set to attend their first class. It just so happened that social studies (their favorite class besides phys. ed.) was first on the agenda. Just before entering the classroom, they prepared themselves for their new experience.

"Well here we go," said Shawn.

"Yeah. Look. That must be our teacher, Mr. Coviello. He looks pretty cool, but he's a lot shorter than I thought he'd be," Brandon observed.

"Man is not known by inches alone, B. Let's check it out."

The boys walked in and saw Mr. Coviello standing behind his desk. He greeted them with a simple nod and a smile, as if to indicate to them that they should sit down and prepare to listen. As they waited for the rest of the class to come in, Brandon studied his new teacher. There was a certain aura about him. Although he was not a man of large physical stature, he seemed to have a presence that exuded authority and commanded respect. He looked like an "all business" type of guy. When the last student entered just before the bell rang, Mr. Coviello slowly walked from behind his desk to the front of the room. He stood there holding his arms behind his back and waited for complete silence. He got it within five seconds. When he was satisfied that he had the undivided attention of the class, he began to address them in his confident, strong voice.

"Good morning everyone. Welcome to Eisenhower Middle School and welcome to the sixth grade. My name is Mr. Coviello, but you may call me 'Mr. C' if you wish. I want you to know that all of your lives just changed the second you walked through my door."

As he spoke, you could hear a pin drop. He paused to absorb the students' reaction, and then began to speak again.

"My social studies class is probably unlike anything you've ever experienced before. Why? Because I see our nation's history as an *adventure*. There are so many fascinating things that have happened in the past, and so many interesting facts that you are probably not aware of. We are going to examine these things very closely, and we should have a lot of fun doing it. However, success in my class requires a lot of hard work and commitment, and like anything else, what you put into it is what you are going to get out of it. Anyway, I think this is going to be a great year, and I'm very excited about it. Once again, welcome. Now, what do you say we get started?"

As Mr. C began to read through the class roster to become familiar with his new students, Brandon knew that he liked his new teacher right away. This was the type of teacher, he thought, that you *wanted* to work hard for. He began to think about all of the cool things he would be studying when suddenly he heard his name called. It completely took him off guard.

"Brandon Morelli?" Mr. C said.

"Here," Brandon responded in a feeble voice.

"Hello, Mr. Morelli. Well, another Italian kid who loves the Yankees, huh? Looks like the two of us have a lot in common already."

Mr. C's greeting made Brandon feel like they had a special bond.

We're both Italian, and we both like the Yankees Brandon thought.

He couldn't keep the smile from his face. But wait a minute! How did Mr. C know that he was a Yankee fan? It was then that Brandon realized he was wearing his favorite Derek Jeter jersey.

When he finished reading the class roster, Mr. Coviello dove right into his teaching. "Okay gang. Here we go. Time to begin our journey through time. We're going to begin with the very beginnings of this land that we call our country. Did you ever wonder who the first people were who lived here?"

"The Indians," a girl in the first row answered after she was called on.

"Okay, the _Native Americans_. But before they came to be known as the 'Native Americans' that we are familiar with, who were these people and where did they come from?"

No one had an answer to offer. Mr. Coviello looked around and then began to explain how thousands of years ago, the early hunters in Asia had to follow their food sources, animals such as mammoths and bison, wherever they migrated. He went on to explain how once there was a land bridge between the continents of Asia and North America, and that the early hunters crossed the bridge hunting for food.

"They were the very first people to set foot on this continent, and they didn't even know it," Mr. C said.

As he continued, Brandon no longer thought of his new teacher as the traditional "teacher." This man was a storyteller. Somehow he was able to get into your head and create images of the things he was talking about. It was like watching some sort of movie in your mind. It was amazing. Mr. C had the whole class in the palm of his hand, each student focused and attentive. When the bell rang at the end of class, Brandon walked over to his pal, Shawn.

"That was cool," he said. "Mr. C's class is already my favorite, and I haven't even been to my other classes yet."

"I know," said Shawn. "I don't think I've ever paid that much attention before."

The boys laughed as they headed for their next class.

Chapter 7

THE FIRST DAY OF SCHOOL had proved to be busy and exhausting. The sixth-graders had met all of their new teachers and had listened to all of their rules and expectations. They took inventory of their new books and materials. And yes, the teachers actually had them reading, writing, and doing homework already. No rest for the weary.

When the dismissal bell rang, the kids lugged their backpacks, which were filled with books, onto the buses that would take them home. As they took their seats, they exchanged observations and stories with one another:

"I can't believe Mr. Morris gave us homework *on the first day!*"

"Did you eat the lunch in the cafeteria? I heard five people got sick from it."

"Doesn't Miss Coffey look like a bird?"

"I was three minutes late for science class because I got lost!"

"Do you think we'll get homework every night in sixth grade?"

"I wish it was still summer."

On and on it went. It was only with each cluster of students being dropped off at their stops did the noise begin to reduce. Shawn, who had been talking with his buddies from the baseball team, gave a nudge to Brandon, who was sitting next to him listening to his MP3 player.

"Brandon. Yo, Brandon!"

"What?" he asked.

"You wanna come over and hang out for a while? Got the game system all set up, and you owe me a rematch in football."

"Sure okay. Let me just call my mom and let her know."

"All right. Cool."

Brandon called his mother on his cell phone and told her he would be over at Shawn's house. She said that was fine, as long as he was home early enough to do his homework and have dinner. As soon as the bus pulled up at their stop, the two of them hopped off and bolted for the front door in a foot race. Everything was a competition for these two. The race was close, but Shawn always seemed to be a bit faster and won the contest.

"Mine!" Shawn yelled as he raised his arms claiming victory.

"That's okay," a heavy-breathing Brandon said, "'cause there's no way you're beating me in football."

"We'll see about that," Shawn replied confidently.

While the boys were in Shawn's room competing for video game glory, Mrs. Thompson walked in, tired from a long day at work.

"Hello boys. How was the first day of school? Did you get any homework?"

"Yeaaaah," the boys dully said as they continued to focus on their game.

"Shawn, are you so locked into that video game that you can't get up and give your mother a kiss?"

"Oh. Sorry mama," Shawn said as he rose and embraced his mother.

"Well thank you," she said. "So tell me about your day. How do you like your new school? What's your favorite class? Who's your favorite teacher? A little information please."

"Everything went okay," Shawn responded. "Math looks like it's going to be tough this year. But the other classes don't seem too bad. Brandon and I really like our new social studies teacher. He seems really cool."

"Great," Mrs. Thompson said enthusiastically. "Tell me about him."

"He's a great guy," Brandon said. "He makes learning about history really interesting. Plus, he's Italian and he's a Yankees fan."

"Can't go wrong with that," Mrs. Thompson said laughing. "Brandon, are you staying for dinner?"

"Yeah," Shawn said. "You wanna stay and eat here?"

"No I can't. I told my mom that I'd be home to get my homework done and have dinner. But thank you Mrs. Thompson."

"You're welcome honey. You know you're welcome any time."

"Well, I guess I better get going. I'll see you tomorrow at school," Brandon said to Shawn.

"All right B. See you tomorrow."

Brandon grabbed his backpack and headed for home on the next block. He had some homework to do and he was tired. It had been a long day. When he got home, he told his mother and father all about his day at school while they ate dinner. They were pleased that he was enthusiastic about his classes and his new school. But then again, Brandon had always been the type of kid who enjoyed school.

"Well you've got the first day of school under your belt," Mr. Morelli told his son. "Once you get that done with, it doesn't take long to get back into the flow."

It turned out Brandon's father was right. It didn't take long at all for Brandon to get back into the routine of school. As classes started to kick into full gear, the days moved by quickly. Eventually those passing days turned into weeks, and the passing weeks turned into months. School was in full swing.

By November, Brandon and Shawn had really settled into Eisenhower Middle School. Both boys were doing well, and they seemed to enjoy all of their classes, especially social studies. In fact, Mr. Coviello's class had been even more enjoyable than Brandon expected. Every day was an adventure, and Brandon quickly developed a passion for learning American history. Whatever Mr. C taught, he wanted to learn more about. Whatever he learned more about had to be investigated further. Hours spent watching television or playing ball after school had been replaced by hours at the computer, researching people, places, and events from the past on the Internet. It simply fascinated him. Every new lesson was a new discovery. However Brandon had no idea that *today's* lesson would lead him back to a discovery he had already made.

Mr. Coviello began class by pulling down an old map of the earth for the students to see. He took a few seconds to pause and look at the map carefully, a silent cue for the class to do the same. When he had finished his observation of the map, he turned to his students.

"Over 500 years ago, this is what people thought the earth looked like. Does anything strike you as unusual about it?"

"There are only three continents," a student in the front of the class observed.

"Yes," said Mr. C. "You will notice that on this map, the earth consists only of Europe, Asia, and Africa. Do you know why the map was drawn this way?"

He looked around the room and saw a hand waving frantically. It belonged to Brandon.

"The people who used this map probably didn't know about the American continents yet. It was a map used before Columbus discovered America," he said.

"Very good Brandon. That's basically true. Before the discovery of the American continents, or the 'New World' as it was later referred to, most people only knew of three continents."

One of Brandon's classmates curiously asked, "What do you mean by *most people*, Mr. C? *Nobody* knew about those continents until Christopher Columbus discovered America, right?"

"Well," answered Mr. Coviello, "it's been mentioned twice so far that Columbus *discovered* America, and this is what is traditionally taught in our history books. There is quite a bit of historical evidence, however, that suggests other discoverers and navigators had come to the New World of the Americas first. Leif Ericsson, for example, was a Norwegian explorer who discovered North America almost 500 years before Columbus's famous voyage. We must also consider the fact that the Native Americans had been living on those continents thousands of years before Columbus arrived. The list goes on and on. Ladies and gentlemen, I'm sorry to be the one to break the news to you, but Christopher Columbus did not *discover* America."

His last statement was like the unveiling of a dark old secret to some of the students, who continued to listen wide-eyed. Immediately several hands were raised to ask the inevitable question that Mr. C knew was coming. A boy named Billy was called on to deliver it.

"If Columbus didn't discover America, why does he get the credit for it, and why do we even celebrate Columbus Day?"

"That's the million-dollar question, isn't it?" Mr. Coviello responded. "Should we no longer celebrate Columbus Day? Should we completely disregard all of his accomplishments? The answer, my friends, is *no*. From a European perspective, Columbus deserves to be celebrated. Why? Because quite frankly, the explorations of the American continents before Columbus were very obscure. No maps were made of these travels, so no one in Europe knew of them. It was *Columbus* who built the bridge between the Old World and the New World. After his famous voyages, *everyone* knew about the new continents. Therefore he gets the credit, the fame, and the glory. However, I'd like all of you to know that his 'discovery' was actually an accident."

The class listened carefully as their teacher pulled down another map in front of the chalkboard. This time, the map displayed the earth as it is known today, with all seven continents.

"When we talk about Columbus and the age of exploration, we are talking about a period of time when navigators had traveled to places they never had before. What we need to ask ourselves is *why* they began to do this. There were several reasons, but the most important among them was *trade*. Has anyone ever heard of Marco Polo?"

"Sure," Shawn offered from his seat in the back. "We played that game at the town pool almost every day over the summer."

Shawn's answer received some laughs from his classmates, including his teacher. Brandon shook his head at his friend in disapproval.

"Well that is a fun game Shawn, and I'm sure many of us wouldn't mind being in the pool playing it right now, but it's not exactly what I'm referring to. I'm talking about Marco Polo the *man*. Anyone ever hear of him?"

Once again, Brandon had his hand up.

"Marco Polo was an explorer, an *Italian* explorer!" He gave extra emphasis to the second part of his answer, mainly to let Mr. C know that Marco Polo shared 'the bond.' Mr.

Coviello chuckled and gave Brandon a nod to acknowledge it.

"Very good Brandon, and you're right, Polo was Italian. But more important, Marco Polo visited the lands of Asia and wrote about his experiences there. He wrote of the people, the customs, and the fine silks and spices that were available there. When he returned and the people of Europe read about the goods that were being traded in Asia, they wanted them for themselves. And so they began to look for sea routes to Asia so they could establish trade there.

"What does all of this have to do with Christopher Columbus?" one of the girls in class asked.

"I'm getting to that Mary," said Mr. C, "and here is your answer."

He walked over to the map, grabbed his pointer, and began to explain.

"Portugal was the first European country to find a sea route to Asia when Vasco da Gama sailed around the southern tip of Africa and reached India. The journey gave Portugal access to the riches of Asia. Now during this period, Spain was a major European power. You can bet that if Portugal had established trade with Asia, Spain was going to also. Little did this country know that their opportunity to do it came in the form of a man named Cristobal Colon. You know him as Christopher Columbus."

Mr. Coviello continued. "In his request to King Ferdinand and Queen Isabella of Spain for sponsorship, Columbus explained that if he and his crew sailed directly west from their country across the Atlantic, he would eventually reach Asia. Remember, at this time, Europeans only knew of three continents, and if what they knew was accurate, Columbus's plan was actually very good. He was well on his way to achieving his goal, but he ran into a big obstacle in the middle of the Atlantic Ocean ... the American continents. His 'discovery' of the Americas was something he never expected. In fact, when he landed in the West Indies, he actually thought he had made it to India. Very simply, my friends, Columbus wasn't looking for new lands. He was looking for a direct sea route to Asia. Therein lays the accident."

Brandon was eating up all of this information. He loved it, and as always, he wanted to learn more. Nervously he raised his hand to ask a question that he hoped his teacher would not regard as silly. When Mr. Coviello acknowledged his raised hand, Brandon asked, "Sailing across the Atlantic seems like a very long trip to make. How did explorers know where they were going in the open sea?"

Mr. C began to nod his head, as if to signify that he approved of the question.

"It seems like that question should be so obvious for us to ask, yet we rarely think about that do we? Explorers used several instruments of navigation to assist them in determining their direction and position. Some of these included the cross-staff, the astrolabe, and the magnetic compass. Unfortunately these instruments weren't always accurate. The astrolabe, for example, measured how high the North Star was above the horizon. From that, you could calculate your latitude. By following the line of latitude, it allowed you to keep a straight course. It was very difficult to maintain, however, because the movement of the ship made the readings uneven. So I suppose you had to be lucky or a good estimator when it came to finding your way in the open seas."

"What happened if your ship hit a rock or sprung a leak while you were in the middle of the ocean?" Mr. C was asked.

"Your ship sank," he quickly responded.

The simplicity of his answer drew laughter from the class.

"Many ships met their end in the middle of the sea. In recent years, scientists and oceanographers have been able to find the wreckage of several old ships on the bottom of the ocean floor. They find all kinds of neat stuff down there."

Brandon imagined all of the fascinating things that could be found from the wreckage of those ships. He actually imagined himself diving to explore the sunken treasures. It would probably be similar to his snorkeling experience over the summer when he found the old watch case. The old watch case! Brandon had totally forgotten about the discovery he had made in the blue waters of the Dominican Republic. He remembered putting the object in his travel bag and not giving it a second thought since.

Perhaps Mr. Coviello would be interested in seeing the case and hearing the story of his find. Yes, that was a good idea. Brandon decided to bring it to school tomorrow to share with his favorite teacher.

Chapter 8

THE NEXT DAY BRANDON FOUND himself doing something he had never done before. He was actually wishing the time away in Mr. Coviello's class. It wasn't that he no longer loved social studies. He just couldn't wait to show Mr. C the old watch case that he had found over the summer. It was burning up in his pocket, waiting to be revealed.

After what seemed like an eternity to Brandon, class finally ended and the bell rang. As the students filed out of the room, Shawn stopped to see why Brandon was lagging behind.

"What's going on, B? You're not in trouble are you?" he asked.

"No, no. You know how Mr. C was talking about the wreckage of old ships and all of the cool things scientists find at the bottom of the ocean yesterday?"

"Yeah."

"Well I thought it would be cool to show him what I found when we went snorkeling at Punta Cana. Remember this?"

Brandon pulled out the old case from his pocket.

"Oh yeah. You still have that old thing? I forgot all about it," Shawn said.

"I did too until Mr. C's lesson yesterday. Come on, I'm going to show him right now."

Brandon and Shawn approached their teacher's desk. Mr. Coviello was looking through some papers when he glanced up and saw the boys.

"Well young explorers, what can I do for you?" The greeting put smiles on both of their faces.

"Mr. C, remember your lesson yesterday when you were talking about the things that scientists find at the bottom of the ocean from old ships?"

"Sure. What about it?"

"Well I have something I want to show you. Over the summer, Shawn and I went with my family to Punta Cana in the Dominican Republic. While we were there, we went snorkeling at El Cortecito Beach."

"Wow. You know, I've always wanted to try that. I've heard it's amazing."

"It is!" Brandon said enthusiastically. "Anyway, while I was free diving looking at the coral reefs, I saw something that looked like it was wedged at the bottom. I wasn't sure what it was, so I went to get a closer look and tried to pry it free. When I did, I came up with this!"

Brandon revealed the case to Mr. C as if he had just pulled a diamond out of his pocket. "It's an old watch case that somebody must have lost a long time ago!"

Curiously and very carefully, Mr. Coviello took the case in his hand. He inspected it thoroughly.

"Hmmm. This looks pretty old. It's probably been in the ocean for quite some time. There also appears to be something engraved on the back of it, but it's hard to tell what it says with all of the wear and tear." He continued to look over the case when suddenly he came to a conclusion about what it might be.

"Brandon, you said this was a watch case? I have to tell you that I think it may be something else. I think this is the case of an old *compass*."

"A compass?" Brandon asked.

"Yes. Of course I'm not completely sure, but I can do some research on it if you'd like. I've had some exposure to the field of archeology, and I've always been interested in old objects. Would you mind if I took this home with me over the weekend?"

"Oh no Mr. C, I wouldn't mind at all. Do you think it might be worth something?"

"That is very tough to determine right now, but you never know. Let me see what I can find out about it, and I'll report back to you with it on Monday. Is that okay?"

"Sure!" the boys said together.

"Okay then. On Monday I'll see the two of you right after school."

"Great! Thanks Mr. C!" Brandon said excitedly.

The two boys had missed the bus to take them home, so they decided to walk. As they did, they couldn't contain their excitement.

"Man, can you imagine if that case you found is worth thousands or even millions of dollars?" Shawn asked. "We'll be rich!"

"And famous!" Brandon added. "We'll be on the front page of every newspaper, and we'll get to be on television! I bet we even get to meet the president of the United States!"

They gave each other a high five and continued to share their fantasies of fame and fortune with one another all the way home.

When Brandon walked through the door of his house, he saw his mother in the kitchen. Immediately he went to tell her the exciting news.

"Mom! Mom!" he yelled.

"Brandon? What is it honey? Is everything okay?"

"Yeah, everything's fine. Guess what! Do you remember that old watch case that I found when we went snorkeling in Punta Cana? Well, I showed it to Mr. Coviello today. He looked at it for a long time, and he thinks that it might be an old *compass* case. He asked if he could take it home to do some research on it."

"Did you let him?" Mrs. Morelli asked.

"Of course!" Brandon replied. "He might find out that the old compass case is actually worth something. Mom, it could be worth thousands, even millions!"

"Whoa, whoa, honey. Slow down a bit. The chances of that old case being worth millions of dollars are very slim. It could turn out to be nothing. Let's just see what Mr. C finds out about it and move on from there, okay?"

"Okay," Brandon said in agreement.

Somehow his mother was always able to put things back in their proper perspective for him. His excitement, however, could not be put in check. The possibility that he had found a lost treasure was still very much alive. So many questions began to run through his head. What exactly was that old object that he found? Who did it belong to? What did the engraving mean on the back of it? He couldn't wait to hear what Mr. C had found out about it. Sleeping was not going to be easy tonight. It might as well have been Christmas Eve for Brandon.

Part 2

A Second Look

Chapter 9

Mr. Coviello was at home sitting at his computer desk, staring at the old case.

The object definitely intrigued him, but now he wasn't exactly sure why he volunteered to investigate it for the boys. It had been a long week, and he was exhausted. More than anything else, he wanted some "R & R time," quiet time to be spent with his wife and fifteen-month-old daughter. Nothing was better than that, and usually, he wouldn't let anything get in the way of it. *So why had he done it?* Perhaps it was because he felt a sense of obligation. John Coviello always had a love for history. People, places, events, and objects from the past simply fascinated him. As a true enthusiast of history with an accomplished education and background, he felt that a student's quest for knowledge *had* to be satisfied. *Feed the hungry minds.* There was no other way for the great Mr. C.

As he closely inspected the case, he decided to use a detective-like approach to his investigation. He began to take notes of its specifications:

Object (compass case?) is in very poor condition. It appears to be made of brass, darkened by time and wear. Size is approximately 32 mm in diameter. The back of the object has something engraved on it. The words "My" and "FIRE" can barely be deciphered. What is the significance of these words? Who can they be linked to?

There were so many questions to answer, so many places for him to begin.

Boy, he thought, *Maybe I should have taken a pass on this one.*

Exhaustion was getting the better of him. A nice warm bed was much more appealing at this point than an old hunk of metal. However, he convinced himself to persevere and carried on. After about ten minutes of fighting frustration and heavy eyelids, it dawned on him. There was someone who could help him with this, an old friend and teacher who had the knowledge and the resources to provide the answers he sought. Of course! Why hadn't he thought of this in the first place? He quickly fumbled through his desk drawers, looking for his personal telephone and address book. When he found it buried under a stack of old papers, he thumbed through it to his desired entry.

Okay, he said to himself, *This should be interesting.*

He picked up the phone and dialed the number. It rang five times without an answer. Just before he was about to hang up thinking that no one was home, a deep, loud voice answered the call.

"Dr. Jonas Stephenson, can I help you?"

"I sure hope so," Mr. Coviello replied. "You've been doing it for the last fifteen years."

"John? John Coviello?" A heavy laugh followed. "Well now, how is my favorite pupil?"

"I'm doing great, Dr. J. How is my all-time favorite teacher?"

"I'm old and fat, John. Yet somehow the Board of Trustees still feels I am of some use around here. Truth be told, life is good. I am truly living the old adage *carpe diem* to its fullest. So many young minds to feed here at the university; so many wonderful things to teach them. You know there's nothing I'd rather be doing."

"Yes, I know all too well. I was one of those young minds at one time, remember?"

"Of course I do. How could I forget the one person I've met in life whose love of history rivaled that of my own? Ah, the long lost son I never had!"

The two men laughed until it was time for Mr. Coviello to make clear his reasons for calling.

"Dr. J, I have something here I need your help with. One of my students found an item of interest while he was vacationing in the Dominican Republic last summer. He showed it to me today and let me take it home this weekend to research. It appears to be the case of an old compass. The condition of the object indicates that it had been under water for quite some time. There is also something engraved on the back of it. It's tough to read, but the words 'my' and 'fire' can be read. I'm not sure, but the boy may have found something significant."

"Significant, you say. That's where *I* come in, right old friend?"

"Well I was hoping you could take a look at it and tell me what you think. You're certainly more qualified to come up with answers than I am."

"It would be my pleasure John. Why don't you stop by tomorrow afternoon and we'll see what we can come up with."

"That sounds great Doc. Thank you. I'll see you tomorrow."

"Indeed," said Dr. Stephenson.

Mr. Coviello hung up the phone feeling a sense of relief and a surge of newfound energy. Tomorrow he would head over to the local university to meet with Dr. Stephenson. Together they would try to uncover the mysteries of the old compass case. Working again with the man who had inspired him like no one else in his life caused him to reflect on his past.

Fifteen years ago John Coviello was a student at the local state university. Having declared himself a history major, he needed to take an elective course for the upcoming spring semester. He decided on Archaeology I. Little did he know it was a course he would come to love. He learned about the excavation and recovery of artifacts, dating techniques, and the interpretation of data. He also examined Old and New World cultures, and learned how archaeology was related to history and other disciplines. All of this was right up his alley. As interesting as he found these aspects to be, however, what John found most interesting about the course was the professor, an eclectic man by the name of Dr. Jonas Stephenson.

Standing at an imposing height of 6 foot 4 and weighing over 250 pounds, Dr. Stephenson looked more like a former NBA basketball player than an archaeology professor. As a matter of fact, his facial features carried a striking resemblance to the great basketball legend Julius Erving, which prompted many of his students to call him "Dr. J." The nickname, which Dr. Stephenson had a great sense of humor about, was made even more humorous by the fact that he knew almost nothing about the game of basketball. _Archaeology_ was his game. This was a man who felt more comfortable with an excavated skull in his hands instead of a basketball, and if you were a student in his class, you were made well aware of it right away. His friendly and engaging personality made Dr. Stephenson a favorite on campus, and he was very well-respected among his peers.

John took an immediate liking to his new professor. It was obvious that this man had a passion for what he taught, and he really knew how to get his students to take an interest in what he was saying. There was no mistaking that Dr. J was a teacher in the true sense of the word, and John was going to absorb as much information from him as he could. Every class he would listen closely to the lectures, ask thought-provoking questions, and comment on things he found interesting. Dr. Stephenson was amazed at young John's enthusiasm and marveled at his knowledge of historical facts. He took an immediate liking to his new student, seeing much of himself in the young man at that age.

Eventually the two of them made a habit of engaging in discussion after every class. They enjoyed each other's company and found that they had quite a bit in common. Most interesting to Dr. Stephenson was the fact that John wanted to become a teacher.

"That is most definitely your calling," Dr. J. once said. "There is a light in you that not everyone has. You need to shine that light on those who hunger for knowledge. *Feed the hungry minds, John.*"

Those words resonated in John Coviello's head ever since.

It was around 1:30 in the afternoon when John saw his old friend and mentor sitting on a campus bench in front of the school library. When he caught sight of his former student, Dr. Stephenson rose to his feet and greeted him with a warm handshake.

"Good to see you my young friend. You look well."

"Thanks Dr. J. It's good to see you too. Thanks for meeting me here today."

"Oh it's my pleasure. Besides, it's been a while since I've seen you. Your teaching duties and that young family of yours must be keeping you busy."

"That's for sure. Seems like time is something I *used* to have."

"I understand John, believe me. Well are you ready to begin our adventure?"

"Yes sir. I have the object right here in my pocket."

"Good. I think the best place for us to start is right here in the library. Let's go."

The two men entered the library and picked out a table in a quiet corner.

"Well here it is, Dr. J. Take a look at this and tell me what you think."

Dr. Stephenson took the case from Mr. Coviello's hand and inspected it very carefully. He studied every angle and every side of the object, nodding his head as if to concur with Mr. Coviello's assessment that his student had indeed found something significant. After what seemed like ten minutes, he finally put the case down on the table with the engraved side up and shared his thoughts.

"Let me begin John by saying that this is, indeed, the case to an old compass. In my studies, I've seen several cases like this that have been brought up from under water excavations, and this one shares the same characteristics. I'm fairly confident about that. Then there is the engraving on the back of the case. It intrigues me for a couple of reasons. First of all, the letters are quite faded, which is an obvious clue that it is quite old. Second, the words that can be deciphered, 'My' and 'FIRE' can give us a clue as to whom this compass might have belonged to. John, I know it's very early to make any conclusions, especially since no dating tests have been administered yet, but this may be the navigational instrument of a fifteenth- or sixteenth-century explorer."

"How in the world can you come to that conclusion already Dr. J? Did I miss something?" Mr. Coviello was incredulous.

"Apparently you have young scholar. Look at the words again. Study them carefully. Now consider what this object is and who would have used it. Put the pieces together. *My*

FIRE. Compass case. Sailors. Explorers. Use that historic mind of yours."

He thought for a very long time, but still came up with nothing. He looked up at Dr. Stephenson's face, which displayed a broad smile, a knowing smile that indicated he had the answer.

"Come on John. I'm not letting you off that easy. You know this."

What in the world was it? What could it be? What was he missing? Dr. Stephenson had given him the clues. *My FIRE. Compass case. Sailors. Explorers. Fire. Fire. FIRE!!!* That was it! He got it! As soon as his eyes widened and he took in the breath of realization, Dr. Stephenson knew he had found the answer.

"St. Elmo's Fire!" John yelled. It was loud enough to turn a few heads in the library.

"That's right my friend. St. Elmo's Fire. Do you remember who wrote about his experience with this phenomenon in his accounts?" The question caused Mr. Coviello's jaw to drop. Could it be? Was it actually possible? Once again he looked across the table and saw that smile on Dr. J's face, only this time he was nodding as if to acknowledge the answer.

"Yes sir Mr. Coviello. I know it's hard to believe, but your student might have found the compass used by Christopher Columbus."

Chapter 10

WHEN MONDAY MORNING FINALLY ARRIVED, Brandon and Shawn got to school early and headed right for Mr. Coviello's room. They had waited all weekend to hear if there was something special about the old case Brandon had found, and they couldn't wait a minute longer. Mr. C was standing in front of a classroom window when the boys arrived, staring outward with a pensive look on his face.

"Hey Mr. C!" Shawn said loudly, taking his teacher by surprise.

"Oh. Good morning gentlemen. I guess having you wait to see me until this afternoon was a futile suggestion. Well I can't say I blame you for coming right away. I probably would have done the same thing."

Brandon didn't waste any time and got right to the point.

"What did you find out Mr. C?"

Mr. Coviello paused and looked at both boys. He then pulled the case out of a protective pouch he had found to keep it safe and held it in his hand.

"Boys," he said, "we have a lot to talk about. I think it is best if we keep to our original plan and meet right after school. That way we can sit down, take our time, and discuss this case. Brandon, would you mind if I held onto this until we see each other this afternoon?"

"I guess not," Brandon replied.

"Good. I'll see the two of you right after school."

After they left Mr. C's classroom, Brandon's head was bursting with questions. "What do you think he found out?" he asked Shawn.

"I don't know, but it must be something important if he needs to tell us *after* school," Shawn replied.

"Yeah it must be. I wonder why he wanted to hold onto the case. Wasn't that strange?"

"Strange? No. That's a good sign B. If Mr. C wants to hold onto the case, he probably wants to keep it safe. Now think. Why would he want it safe? I'll tell you why ... *the case is probably worth something.*"

A big smile quickly formed on Shawn's face.

"You're right Shawn! It all adds up! Oh man, I can't believe it! I actually found something valuable! What do you think it's worth?"

"I'm not sure. It could be that Mr. C isn't sure at this point either. Let's see what he has to say after school."

Later that afternoon, Mr. Coviello dismissed his last class for the day and waited for the boys to arrive. While he waited, he decided that he had to be very careful about what he told them. It was true that Dr. Stephenson's theory about the engraving on the back of the compass case being directly linked to Christopher Columbus was very exciting, but nothing had actually been proven yet. *Therefore,* he thought, *revealing this theory to the boys would be premature and possibly dangerous.* He would tell them only the *facts* about the case at this time, nothing more. When the boys entered the room, they were breathing heavily, an obvious sign that they had run all the way from their last classroom to his.

Mr. C looked at the two of them, shook his head, and said, "Gentlemen, I take it the two of you are aware that this school has rules against running in the hallways."

As the three of them sat down at a table in the back of his classroom, Mr. C found that he was actually a little nervous. Holding onto a navigational instrument that possibly belonged to the most famous explorer in history could do that to anybody. Did the boys notice? He hoped not. After taking a deep breath, he began to address them.

"Okay gentlemen, as you know, I took the case home over the weekend to find out what I could about it. I thought I would be able to find a great deal of information on my own, but I was wrong."

When he said this, Brandon's face dropped with a look of utter defeat. It was as if someone had let all of the air out of his balloon. His teacher was quick to pick up on this, and held up his hand to signify that there was more to tell.

"*However,*" he said, "I am not one to give up so easily." This put a smile back on Brandon's face and hope back into his spirit. Mr. Coviello continued.

"So I called an old friend of mine to help me out. Truth be told, he's actually more than a friend. He's my old archaeology professor from college. His name is Dr. Stephenson, and he is a brilliant man. Dr. Stephenson and I sat down at the library on campus and studied the case. We were able to come up with some interesting theories about it."

"What is it Mr. C? Please tell us!" Brandon was about to burst with excitement.

"Okay Brandon, calm down, and I'll be happy to tell you. First of all, Dr. Stephenson confirmed that this is indeed, a compass case. He has seen quite a few of them in his studies, so he was able to determine that almost immediately."

"Cool," said Shawn. "Did it belong to someone famous, like an explorer?" he looked over at Brandon and the excitement began to build.

"We don't know that yet Shawn. But that possibility certainly exists. That being said, I want the two of you to keep in mind that Dr. Stephenson and I conducted very *basic* research over the weekend. There were no scientific or chemical tests done on the case to determine its age, so anything is possible."

"You mean that it could be that the case is only fifty years old?" Brandon asked.

"It could be," Mr. C. replied. "We have to keep our minds open and realistic about all of the possibilities."

This brought the boys back down to earth. What if the compass case *was* only fifty or a hundred years old? It would certainly make it a lot less valuable, and realistically, it was the most likely scenario. As Brandon and Shawn gave considerable thought to this, Mr. Coviello grabbed their attention with what he said next.

"Boys, I'm not done yet. I think the next piece of information that I have to share might interest you. It has to do with the engraving on the back of the compass case."

This indeed got their immediate attention. The meaning of the words that had been engraved on the case was a mystery that had been unsolved since Brandon found it.

"If you remember," Mr. C continued, "the words 'My' and 'FIRE' appear on the back of the case. Dr. Stephenson and I tried to determine the significance of these words and how they might relate to a navigational instrument like a compass. What we found out, well, what *he* found out, was very interesting. Believe it or not, the word 'fire' may have a connection to sea navigation and exploration."

"How?" Brandon asked inquisitively. "Did a lot of ships catch fire while they were at sea?"

"From a certain perspective, the answer to your question is yes, Brandon. But it's not the literal 'fire' that you may be thinking of. The inscription 'My Fire' on the back of the case may refer to St. Elmo's Fire."

"Elmo?" Shawn asked incredulously. "You mean the little red guy from *Sesame Street*? What does *he* have to do with all of this?"

"Absolutely nothing Shawn. You've got the wrong Elmo. St Elmo is also known as Saint Erasmus, the patron saint of sailors."

"Where does the *fire* come from?" Brandon asked.

"Here's the answer Brandon." Mr. C took out a sheet of paper with something written on it.

"Since you know that I am not a man of science, I thought it would be better if I wrote this down so I could include all of the scientific terminology. Here it goes. St. Elmo's fire is *an electro luminescence coronal discharge caused by the ionization of the air during thunderstorms inside of a strong electric field.*"

The boys paused for a moment to absorb the meaning of what he had just said. Then Shawn, seeking clarification said, "So it's like lightning during a thunderstorm, right?"

"Pretty much," said Mr. C. "It is a phenomenon that occurs at the mastheads of ships during thunderstorms at sea. It's generally regarded as a good omen."

"So the words 'My Fire' refer to St. Elmo's Fire, and this happens on ships at sea. That's interesting Mr. C, but how does this help us find out who the compass belonged to?"

Brandon's question put a smile on Mr. Coviello's face because it was the type of question he himself would have asked at that age. But the smile quickly disappeared when he realized the question was leading him to a place he didn't want to go yet. He had to be very careful about how he answered. Revealing too much would cause the boys to overreact, thinking they had discovered one of the greatest treasures in history. There would be a frenzy caused in the school, in the town, and in the personal lives of everyone who was involved with this. Even though there was a possibility that they had indeed found something special, it was way too early for that. Mr. Coviello put on a serious face and began to answer Brandon.

"There have been several men in history who have written about the phenomenon, some from personal experience and some as part of fictional literature."

"Who?" Brandon inevitably asked.

"The list is long and distinguished. Great men like Benjamin Franklin, Henry Wadsworth Longfellow, Christopher Columbus, and even William Shakespeare have all made references to —"

"Christopher Columbus?" Brandon couldn't help interrupting. "What did *he* write about it?"

The sudden interest in Columbus made Mr. Coviello uneasy because the famous explorer was the one Dr. Stephenson directly linked to the compass. There was no way he was going to let them know that, so he told them the basic facts.

"Columbus wrote about it in the account of his second voyage. He and his crew had experienced the flashes of light during a pretty strong thunderstorm. Although he described the storm as frightful, he stated with certainty that when St. Elmo appeared, there could be no danger. He saw it as a good omen."

"Wait a minute Mr. C," Shawn said, "is it possible that this compass belonged to Christopher Columbus?"

"Possible, Shawn? Yes. Likely? The odds are long against it. Like I said, no tests have been done to date the object yet. Plus, even if it was determined that this was an instrument from the fifteenth century, we would have to find conclusive evidence that this did indeed belong to Columbus."

"Mr. C, do you think we can get this compass dated?" Brandon asked. "I really want to know if it is from Columbus's time."

"I'm glad you asked me that Brandon, because I was going to ask you if I could take it back to the university to conduct more research on it."

"Of course! I want you to find out as much as you can!"

"Yeah," said Shawn. "It seems like there's so much more to do."

"There is," said Mr. Coviello, "but it's going to take some time. Let me give Dr. Stephenson a call tonight and tell him that the owner of this artifact and his associate have given me express permission to conduct more research."

The statement brought smiles and laughter from the boys. Mr. Coviello extended his hand to each of them, giving a hearty handshake. He was happy with the way things went. He told Brandon and Shawn what they needed to know without filling them with false hope or hysteria. The problem, he found, was that he could not provide the same comfort for himself.

Chapter 11

"CAN IT REALLY BE THIS easy?" Mr. Coviello thought to himself as he sat with the compass case in his office at home.

It seemed that the object had been linked to Columbus so easily, yet something wasn't clicking with him. Before he called Dr. Stephenson at the university to make arrangements for another round of researching, he wanted to spend some time looking at the engraving on the back of the case on his own. Everyone who had seen the compass had been able to decipher the words "My FIRE," but because of the wear and tear the object had sustained, it took a good hard look to make those words out. That concerned him a bit. But there was something else about the words that really bothered him. *The two words were not located in the center of the case.* If these were the only two words that were engraved, shouldn't they have been centered? Why were they located to the lower-right of the case? Was there something else that had been scratched off by the corals when Brandon pulled it out?

Mr. C decided that he needed to get a closer look at the case. From one of his desk drawers, he retrieved a large magnifying glass. Slowly and carefully, he looked at the words. The "M" and "y" in the word "My" seemed to be fairly clear, but when he examined the word "FIRE" something was wrong. As he focused on the letter "I" in the word, he found that it was not actually an "I" … it was an "E"! Apparently the three small horizontal lines in the letter had been so faded they could hardly be seen by the naked eye.

"Oh no," he said out loud.

The revelation was like a punch to the gut. Every ounce of excitement and enthusiasm that had once been in him was drained by this new discovery. The theory about St. Elmo's Fire and its link to Columbus no longer applied to the compass. How disappointing. *The boys*, he thought, *will be crushed when they hear the news.*

Where did they go from here? Mr. C wasn't sure. He didn't know what to make out of the engraving that now read "My FERE." That didn't seem to make any sense, which reaffirmed to him that there had to be something more on the case. With this thought in mind, he once again began to examine the entire surface where the engraving was. To the far left of "FERE" he vaguely made out the letter "X." Right above the letter "X," he found what looked to be the letter "S." As he scanned the rest of the surface, he found that no other letters could be found. Mr. C took out a piece of paper and wrote down all of the letters in the exact locations that they appeared on the compass case.

What is this? he asked himself. *Looks like we have a whole new mystery to solve here.*

With that, he picked up the phone and called Dr. Stephenson, telling him everything that he had discovered using the magnifying glass.

"How unfortunate," Dr. Stephenson said when Mr. C was finished.

"I know," Mr. Coviello replied. "I was really hoping we had something here."

"We still might John. Remember, we came to a conclusion about the engraving based only on a theory. We didn't conduct any hard research. Your new discoveries present us with a whole new challenge, and you know how much I love a good challenge."

"I sure do, and I think that's just what you're going to get with this. I can't figure out what in the world this engraving means now. I'm totally befuddled."

"Well we can't have that now can we? Why don't you come here on Saturday with the compass and we'll continue our research."

"Okay. I just have to get permission from my wife."

"Do you want me to talk to her John?"

"It was just a joke Dr. J."

"Oh. Very well then. I'll see you Saturday."

"See you Saturday."

As he hung up the phone, Mr. Coviello thought about how he was going to break the news to Brandon and Shawn. He knew it wasn't going to be easy, but they had to know the truth.

The next day the boys came into social studies class only to find Mr. C wearing a peculiar look on his face. He was smiling, but it seemed there was no happiness behind the smile. Brandon knew that look. It was the expression his mother would put on whenever his baseball team lost a game. It was the "I'm sorry" look. What had happened? He had to know. He immediately approached his teacher and asked if everything was okay. Mr. Coviello gave the dreaded response, "See me after school."

Great, Brandon thought, *Another day of being unable to concentrate on anything but this dumb compass.*

It was only second period. Waiting the whole day to find out what was troubling Mr. Coviello would be torture. He needed to talk to someone. Not surprisingly, he turned to the only person who could relate: Shawn.

"Something's wrong," he said.

"What's the matter?"

"I'm not sure, but it looks like Mr. C found out something bad about the compass."

"Are you sure? He looks fine to me."

"Yeah I'm sure. Didn't you see the look on his face when we came in?"

"Guess I wasn't really paying attention. Listen B, are you sure you're not getting carried away with this whole thing? Seems like you've become obsessed."

"I have! And so have *you* Shawn! Don't even try to pretend that you're not! Yesterday you kept talking about having season tickets to Yankee games for the rest of your life if we became rich. You're an—"

"Boys!" Mr. Coviello said sternly from the front of the classroom. "If you don't mind I'd like to begin my lesson now. As a matter of fact, why don't the two you see me after school and we'll discuss the procedures that are involved with getting ready for class."

While the rest of the students in class interpreted Mr. C's remarks as disciplinary in nature, Brandon and Shawn knew that their teacher was saying in a clever way, "Save the discussion for this afternoon."

After eighth period, the boys returned to Mr. Coviello's room. He motioned for them to take a seat at the table in the back of the room once again. Without wasting any time, he got right down to business.

"I'm afraid I have some bad news gentlemen. The engraving on the back of the compass isn't what we thought it was."

"You mean it's not St. Elmo's Fire?" Shawn asked.

"It's not *anyone's* fire Shawn."

"What do you mean?" Brandon asked.

"Here's what happened," Mr. C. said. "When I took the compass case home last night, I wanted to take another close look at the engraving. In doing so, I found that there were some things that didn't sit right with me. Here, take a look at it again carefully. If the words "My FIRE" are the only words engraved on the case, why is it that they aren't centered? See how they are located to the bottom right? It doesn't make sense."

The boys nodded in agreement.

"This led me to take a look at the words more carefully. You'll notice that the letters from the words that we have deciphered are very worn and hard to read."

"We knew that already Mr. C. How docs this prove the engraving isn't what we thought it was?" Brandon asked.

Mr. Coviello pulled out his magnifying glass.

"Here," he said. "I want each of you to focus on the 'I' in the word 'FIRE.' Look closely and tell me what you see."

The boys took the magnifying glass from their teacher and looked at the letter in the word. After a few seconds, their eyes went from squinting to wide.

"It's not an 'I'; it's an 'E'!" Shawn observed.

"That's right. It's actually an 'E.' You couldn't see it without using magnification. So you see, what we thought was the word fire, actually isn't. It seems that our theory about St. Elmo's Fire and its possible link to Christopher Columbus do not apply to this compass anymore."

"I knew this whole thing was too good to be true," said Brandon.

"Hold on Brandon. Our study of this object isn't over yet. As a matter of fact, I still plan to meet with Dr. Stephenson this weekend to see if we can find out something about this artifact. C'mon fellas. You know the game isn't over until the last out. We're still in the game!"

Chapter 12

ON SATURDAY AFTERNOON, MR. COVIELLO met Dr. Stephenson at the university. Once again they headed to the library on campus to study the compass.

"Well John, are you ready to take another stab at this wonderful adventure in archaeology?" Dr. Stephenson asked.

"I sure am," he responded.

"Good. Did you bring the notes you took from your last observation?"

"Yes I did. I think you'll find them quite interesting."

Mr. C took out his notebook and opened to the section where he had written his notes. He then handed them to an eager Dr. Stephenson.

"Well," he said, "this certainly changes the game a bit, doesn't it? Very interesting."

"Yes it is," Mr. C said. "If you notice, I was able to decipher two more letters at the left side of the compass case. There appears to be an 'S' at the top and an "X" at the bottom, next to the word we thought was 'fire.' There are also some other markings that I don't know what to make of."

"I see. Well unlike the last time we met, I don't have any earth-shattering theories as to what this means. It's obvious from your use of the magnifying glass that there was much more engraved on this case than we originally thought. Much of it appears to have been scratched off. That doesn't make our job very easy, does it?"

"No Dr. J. It sure doesn't. Where do we begin with something like this?"

"Why don't we begin by doing something that will give us an idea of what period this object came from?"

"You want to conduct _dating tests_ first?"

"Why not? All of the resources we need to do this are at our disposal right here at the university. The tests will at least give us some answers as opposed to just theories. Of course you would have to leave the compass with me for a few days. Would that be okay?"

"I'd have to call my student, Brandon, and ask him. It's _his_ compass. If he gives me the okay, then we're on."

"Of course. Call your student and let me know what he says. Now since there's nothing more for us to do here today, go home to your family. You shouldn't be spending all of your Saturdays with old college professors."

"Okay Doc. I'll call him as soon as I get home. If all goes well, I'll drop the compass off at your office on Monday."

"Very well John. A pleasure working with you again."

"As always sir."

With that, the two men left the library and headed home.

When Mr. Coviello arrived home, he went to his briefcase to find his class lists with his students' addresses and phone numbers on them. He thumbed through until he found his desired class—6B. Scanning down the list of students, he wrote down the home phone number of Brandon Morelli on a piece of paper and took it to the phone.

"Who are you calling honey?" his wife asked from the baby's room.

"I have to call one of my students to ask if Dr. Stephenson can run some tests on that old compass I was telling you about the other day."

"Still haven't come up with anything yet huh?

"Nope. Not yet. Well let's see if I get the okay."

He dialed the number to Brandon's home and waited for an answer. After three rings, someone picked up.

"Hello?"

"Hello, Mr. Morelli? This is John Coviello from Eisenhower Middle School. I'm Brandon's social studies teacher."

"Oh of course. How are you Mr. Coviello? I've got to tell you, my son just *loves* your class. Besides baseball, it seems that's all he talks about."

"Well it's always nice to hear things like that. I appreciate it. Brandon is a terrific kid and a very bright student."

"Thank you Mr. Coviello. Was there something I can help you with?"

"Actually yes. My call is in regard to the compass case that Brandon brought in."

"Oh yes. I heard that there was a bit of a letdown with the case the other day. The engraving didn't actually say 'fire' I was told."

"No it didn't. I know Brandon was very disappointed, as I was. It's just one of those things that happen when you try to find out information about artifacts. Anyway, the reason why I'm calling is because I wanted to ask Brandon if we could run some dating tests on the compass at the university. I don't know if he told you, but an old friend of mine is an archaeology professor there, and he has access to several resources we can use to study the object."

"Yes he did mention that. Unfortunately Brandon's not home right now. He's off playing with Shawn somewhere. However, if you need to run tests on that old case, you go right ahead. I know my son wouldn't have a problem with it at all."

"Are you sure Mr. Morelli?"

"Absolutely. I'm kind of interested myself to see what you can come up with."

"Me too. I'd be lying if I said I didn't share in the kids' excitement."

"Well good luck, Mr. Coviello. I'm sure Brandon will fill me in on what you found."

"I'm sure he will. Thank you so much for your help Mr. Morelli. It was nice talking to you."

"Same here. Take care now."

"Bye-bye."

Mr. C had gotten the permission he sought. On Monday he would drop off the compass to Dr. Stephenson.

Chapter 13

IN THE MIDDLE OF THE week, Brandon stopped by Mr. Coviello's room before first period to chat with his favorite teacher. It seemed as though he was doing this routinely ever since he and Shawn introduced the compass to him.

"What's up Mr. C? Have you heard from Dr. Stephenson yet?"

It had been two days since the compass was brought to the university to be tested.

"Not yet Brandon. However, I'm sure that I'll be hearing from him very soon. Don't worry. Hey, did you happen to watch the Yankee game last night? Boy what a slug-fest! I would have loved to have been at the stadium for *that* one!"

Mr. C could see that Brandon was very stressed out about the compass. Anything he could do to get the boy's mind off of it for a while was worth a try.

"Yeah," Brandon said unenthusiastically, "Some game." It didn't work.

"Look Brandon, I know how disappointed you are about the compass. Finding out that the engraving on the back was something other than what we originally thought was a letdown for *all* of us."

"I know. I guess I let myself get carried away with the whole thing a little too much. I just thought I had something very special. Christopher Columbus is one of my favorite historical figures. To think that I might've found something that actually belonged to him was amazing."

"I know what you mean," Mr. C. said. "Columbus is one of my favorites too."

"Really?" Brandon asked. "What do you like most about him Mr. C?"

"There are so many things to admire about the man. But I think what intrigues me the most about him are the many mysteries that surround him."

"Mysteries? What mysteries?"

"The list is long my young scholar. Columbus was a man history remembers as the world's most famous explorer, yet there are so many things about him that are shrouded in mystery and controversy. I'll give you an example. Tell me Brandon, where is Christopher Columbus from?"

"Oh come on Mr. Coviello! That's easy. He's an Italian!"

"From Genoa, right? Yes, that's what the history books teach you, and that is what is most widely accepted. However, there is a great deal of evidence that suggests Columbus was not Italian at all. He may have been a Catalan."

"A what?"

"A Catalan. Back in the fifteenth century, Catalonia was a region of Spain, before Spain was the nation that we are familiar with today. It was a separate territory with its own culture and its own laws. Sorry to disappoint you my fellow Italian, but Columbus probably didn't share our ethnic heritage."

"How do you know that for sure?"

"I don't know for sure. Like everyone else, all I can do is study the evidence that is out there and form my own opinion from it. Consider this Brandon. In preserved documents, Columbus wrote almost exclusively in Spanish with Catalan phonetics. He used this language even when he wrote personal notes to himself. What does that tell you? If he was Italian, wouldn't it make sense that he wrote in *Italian*? Little clues like this sometimes provide big answers."

"That's pretty interesting. I've never heard of Catalonia before. What other mysteries can you tell me about?"

"*Tell* you about? No. This next mystery I will *show* you." Mr. Coviello went to the bookshelf and took out an encyclopedia. When he found his desired page, he called Brandon over to look at it.

"Here," he said, "take a look at this."

Brandon looked at the page and saw the iconic portrait of Christopher Columbus painted by Sebastiano del Piombo. Mr. C let his student take a few seconds to get a good look at the picture.

"Who is that a portrait of?" he asked.

"Christopher Columbus," Brandon answered.

"Are you sure?"

"Wait a minute Mr. C. Are you going to tell me that's *not* Christopher Columbus?"

"I will tell you that it is *meant* to be him, but the truth is, although there is a great deal of artwork that involves Columbus as its subject, no authentic portraits of the man were ever painted in his lifetime." Brandon's eyes began to widen.

"That's right. We don't know exactly what Christopher Columbus looked like. Artists who painted portraits of him after his death used written descriptions to construct his appearance. Believe it or not, it happens to be the truth."

"That's incredible!" Brandon exclaimed.

"It sure is. But what may be even more incredible is the controversy concerning his final resting place."

"You mean we don't even know where he is buried?"

"Yes and no. When Columbus died, his body underwent excarnation."

"What is that?" Brandon asked.

"It's when the flesh is removed from the body so that only the bones remain. Anyway, his body, or what was left of it, traveled to different places before a final resting place was found. When he first died, his body was interred in Spain, first in the city of Valladolid and then at a monastery in Seville. A short time later, his son Diego wanted the remains of his father moved to Santo Domingo, which is in the Dominican Republic."

"Why did he want them moved *there*?"

"Because Diego had been the governor of Hispaniola, and he wanted his father to be with him. Now here's where it gets a little crazy. About 250 years after the remains were brought to the Dominican Republic, the French took over and removed them. They ended up in Havana, Cuba. One hundred years later, after the Spanish-American War, the remains were moved back to the Cathedral of Seville, where they were placed on a decorative catafalque."

"What's a catafalque?" Brandon wondered.

"It's a raised platform used to support a coffin or casket. Would you like to see a picture of it?" Mr. C asked.

"Sure!" his student said excitedly.

Mr. Coviello opened another book from his shelf and offered it to Brandon. "Here," he said, "take a look."

"Wow. That's really cool. I really like the four soldiers that are holding up the coffin."

"They're not soldiers Brandon. They are the heralds of the four nations that united under King Ferdinand and Queen Isabella of Spain. Amazing isn't it?"

"Yeah. How do you know about all of this stuff Mr. C?"

"Very simple: I *read*. You don't get a lot of this stuff on television."

"No I guess not. So if this is the tomb where Columbus's remains are, what is the controversy about?"

"Well a little over a hundred years ago, a lead box was found in Santo Domingo that had an inscription identifying

'Don Christopher Columbus' on it. It contained fragments of bone inside. There were many who believed that the remains in that lead box might have been those of Columbus."

"So we don't know if Columbus's remains are in Spain or the Dominican Republic?"

"The answer to that question has been *partially* answered for us. Only a few years ago, DNA samples were taken from the remains in Seville. It was found that at least *some* of those remains belonged to Columbus."

"Some? What about the rest of him?"

"We don't know. The authorities in Santo Domingo have not allowed DNA testing on the remains that are in their possession. Until they do, we won't know if Christopher Columbus's remains rest in one place or two. It continues to be a mystery."

Brandon shook his head incredulously.

"I can't believe it. All of those things that you told me about Columbus are amazing. I had no idea there were so many mysteries about him. You never see this stuff in the social studies books."

"I know. Sometimes if you want to find the good stuff, you have to go a step or two beyond what you have. *If you dig deep and you don't find anything, dig deeper.* That is something I learned from Dr. Stephenson when I was *his* student. The information is out there Brandon. You just have to look for it."

"Dr. Stephenson must have been a pretty cool teacher, huh?"

"Yes he was. I learned a great deal from him."

"Well I've already learned a great deal from you Mr. C, and I'm not even finished with sixth grade yet!"

"Thank you Brandon. I have a feeling you're going to learn much more before the year is through. Now it's almost time for the homeroom bell. You better get out of here and get your books ready for class. I'll see you for social studies."

"Okay Mr. C. Thanks for telling me all of that stuff about Columbus."

"You're very welcome. And remember, as soon as I hear from Dr. Stephenson, I'll let you know immediately."

Chapter 14

IT WAS THURSDAY AFTERNOON WHEN Mr. Coviello received the call he had been waiting for at his home.

"Hello John. This is Dr. Stephenson."

Finally! "What's up Dr. J? I've been waiting for your call."

"I'm sure you have. The results from the dating tests we conducted on the compass case just came in and they are quite fascinating. I'd like to share them with you in person if that's okay. Could I come over to the school tomorrow afternoon?"

"Sure you can! I finish with classes around 3:00. Come by around then."

"Fine. I'd also like you to invite the two young men who found the case. I would very much like to meet them."

"I certainly will. I've told them a lot about you, so I'm sure they're very anxious to meet you too."

"Great. I look forward to it. See you tomorrow."

"Okay Dr. J. See you tomorrow."

Mr. Coviello hung up the phone with a renewed sense of excitement and wonder. He knew that Dr. Stephenson must have found out something very significant about the case for him to request a meeting in person. Why else would he make that request? And why else would he want to meet Brandon and Shawn? It had to be something big! This was terrific! The adventure surrounding the mystery of the compass case had not ended with the misreading of the engraving. A new adventure was about to begin!

The next morning at school, Mr. Coviello flagged down Brandon and Shawn in the hallway.

"Boys," he said, "I'd like the two of you to come by my classroom today after school. We have some new information about the compass, and there is someone coming by who would like to meet you."

"Dr. Stephenson finally called?" Brandon asked excitedly.

"Yes he did Brandon. As a matter of fact, *he's* the person coming by who wants to meet the two of you."

"What did the tests say Mr. C?" asked Shawn.

"To be perfectly honest with you Shawn, I don't know. Dr. Stephenson wouldn't tell me over the phone. He wanted to tell all of us in person."

"It must be good news then," Brandon observed.

"Yeah, that's what I thought too." Mr. Coviello said. "Anyway, come by right after school and we'll all find out for sure."

"Okay Mr. C!" the boys said in unison.

There was a glow that returned to the boys' faces as they looked at each other incredulously. Dr. Stephenson was coming by to deliver what was certain to be exciting news. Yes! The magic was back! The boys felt as if they were walking on air as they made their way down the hallway to their first-period class.

"I knew it!" Brandon exclaimed to Shawn. "I knew there was something special about that case!"

Brandon wasn't exaggerating. Since the time he had revealed it to Mr. Coviello, he had felt some strange connection to the old compass. Deep down within himself, he knew there was a reason why he had found the object in the calm blue waters of the Dominican Republic. There *had* to be something special about it! Surely this was why fate had chosen him.

"This is really cool B. I wonder how far back that compass goes," Shawn said.

"I don't know Shawn, but we're gonna find out!"

With that, the two boys entered the room for their first class. It was going to be a great day … a day they would never forget.

Chapter 15

IT HAD BEEN A LONG haul of classes at Eisenhower Middle School. Brandon and Shawn were exhausted from the endless hours of reading, taking notes, reviewing problems, and completing class work. Still, their excitement could not be contained. When the bell rang at the conclusion of their last class, they headed right for Mr. Coviello's room. Big news awaited them, including a meeting with Dr. Stephenson, the man who had been studying the compass case with Mr. C.

On entering the classroom, the boys noticed a very large figure talking to their teacher at his desk. He was an older gentleman, but to the boys he appeared to be a giant. He absolutely towered over Mr. C. Could this be the great Dr. Stephenson?

"Ah, boys!" Mr. Coviello greeted them warmly. "Come on in." Mr. C motioned to each one of them. "Brandon Morelli and Shawn Thompson, allow me to introduce you to my favorite teacher and my very good friend, Dr. Jonas Stephenson."

"It's a pleasure to meet you boys. I've heard a lot about you," Dr. Stephenson said as he shook both of their hands.

"Yeah, it's nice to meet you too," said Shawn who gazed upward. He followed his greeting with the inevitable question that was always asked of Dr. Stephenson.

"Did you ever play in the NBA?"

The question prompted Mr. Coviello and Dr. Stephenson to look at each other and engage in a hearty laugh.

"No son," Dr. Stephenson replied, "I'm not really interested in basketball. I've always had more of an interest in archaeology."

"Dr. Stephenson is asked that question all the time Shawn. Given his size, you'd think he would have chosen to pursue success in that sport, but I assure you, he made the right choice in his career path. This man is one of the finest archaeology professors you will ever meet."

"Well thank you John. I appreciate that. And I think it's only appropriate to tell the two of you that your teacher was one of my finest students. He was an intellectual superstar in the classroom, and I'm proud to say that I helped convince him to use those skills to become a teacher. It seemed to have worked out for him."

Dr. Stephenson took a moment to pause and regain focus on the task at hand.

"Now," he said, "I think we've spent enough time exchanging pleasantries gentlemen. What do you say we talk about this old compass case?" It was precisely what Brandon was thinking.

"Dr. Stephenson, how old is the case that I found? What did you find out?" Brandon asked impatiently.

"Well Brandon, let me begin by telling you that when an archaeologist has the task of dating a metal such as bronze, the process can be very difficult."

"Don't you do that carbon dating thing with artifacts that you find?" Brandon asked.

"Not on *all* artifacts. Carbon-14 dating, which is what I believe you are referring to, is a process that is applicable only to matter that was *living* at one time. Things such as cloth, wood, bone, and plant fibers are ideal for this type of testing because they all take in carbon dioxide from the air. *Metal* samples such as brass do not act as good samples to do this kind of testing on."

"So how do you find out how old things made of metal are?" Shawn asked inquisitively. "Are there other tests that you can do?"

"As a matter of fact, yes Shawn. While few tests can produce results with 100 percent accuracy, there are some tests that can give us fairly reliable data. Cross dating tests, for example, tell us an artifact that is dated at one archaeological site will be of the same age if it is found elsewhere. Ever hear of that before?"

"Nope," Shawn said.

"Well we also use relative dating tests, which examine the relation of the date of anything found to the date of other things found in its immediate neighborhood. It's simply dating by comparing. Finally there is absolute dating, which is the process of determining a specific date for an artifact. This type of dating uses historical records and the analysis of biological and geological patterns that result from climatic variations.

"Which test did you use on the compass case?" Brandon inquired.

"We used a variety of tests Brandon, including the ones that I just mentioned. Unfortunately the results of these tests did not supply us with a totally conclusive date for the compass. However we were able to get what many sports enthusiasts would call a ballpark estimate."

"Well? What is it?" Mr. Coviello asked his former teacher. His impatience matched that of his two students. "What's the estimated age of the compass?"

"We believe the age of the compass case falls somewhere between the fifteenth and sixteenth centuries John."

There was a long pause before anyone spoke. It was as if the three individuals who heard the news for the first time needed at least ten to fifteen seconds to absorb the information. Finally Mr. Coviello broke the silence.

"That's incredible," he said. "I never thought it would have dated that far back. Unbelievable!"

"Believe it my friend. It seems this young man made quite a find," Dr. Stephenson said referring to Brandon.

"He sure did," Shawn said. "So how much money do you think it's worth? Thousands? *Millions*?"

Dr. Stephenson began to chuckle.

"Whoa. Slow down for a minute son. Unfortunately the discovery of old artifacts doesn't automatically translate into instant riches. If it did, I would have retired a long time ago. There is still a great deal about this object that has to be explored. For example, we don't know who it belonged to, we don't know where it was made, and we still haven't figured out the significance of the engraving on the back of it. To say that we still have a lot of work to do before we plan on opening Swiss bank accounts for ourselves is an understatement."

Dr. Stephenson's response to Shawn brought the boys back to earth. It was certainly true that the estimated age of the case was cause for celebration and excitement, but to make any attempt at attaching a dollar value to it at this point was very premature. For the case to have any real value, it had to be attached to a famous person, place, or event. Right now they couldn't attach the object to anyone or anything, famous or otherwise.

"The information we have from this compass case is very limited," Mr. Coviello said. "We need some sort of key to unlock the mysteries behind it. I believe that key lies within the engraving on the back. Brandon, if it's okay with you, I'd like to hold onto the case to take another look at the engraving. Maybe I can find out *something* that will give us some answers."

"Okay," Brandon said confidently. "If anyone can find out what that engraving says, it's you Mr. C."

The faith that the young man had put in his teacher brought a proud smile to the face of Dr. Stephenson. It was obvious that his former student had the one thing that all teachers need from their students in order to be effective — trust.

"I think you've made a wise decision Brandon," Dr. Stephenson said. "Mr. Coviello has a special knack for solving puzzles and unlocking mysteries. He's always been gifted that way. Give him some time, and I'm sure he will come up with something we can use."

"Thanks Dr. J. I'll certainly do my best," Mr. C. replied.

"_Dr. J?_" Shawn asked in a perplexed manner. "Doesn't Dr. Stephenson's last name begin with an S? I'm confused."

"The nickname has nothing to do with his last name Shawn. You're too young to remember him in his playing days, but before Michael Jordan and Shaq ruled the NBA, there was a man by the name of Julius Erving who revolutionized the game of basketball. He was known to everyone as Dr. J. The good doctor here has a striking physical resemblance to him, so many of his students from my generation refer to him as Dr. J. There's a lot of ironic humor to this name since Dr. Stephenson couldn't care less about basketball."

Both boys began to laugh.

"Do you get mad when people call you that Dr. Stephenson?" Shawn asked.

"Not at all Shawn. As a matter of fact, if the two of you would like to call me that, you are more than welcome to. After all, that's how all of my friends refer to me."

The boys looked at each other and smiled. This great man who had taught Mr. C was actually inviting the two of them to be his friends. They both felt a sense of honor.

"Well," Brandon said, "I guess we better get going. Thanks, Mr. C. Very nice meeting you … Dr. J."

"The pleasure was all mine Brandon. I'm sure we'll be meeting again to talk about that old compass. I look forward to it. Take care now."

Dr. Stephenson shook hands with both Brandon and Shawn as they made their way out. He had been impressed with both of them.

"Fine young scholars you have there John," he said.

"Yes they are. Real good kids."

"Well I guess I had better get going too. Best of luck in your endeavors to decode that engraving," Dr. Stephenson said. "If you need me for anything, just call."

"I will Doc. Thanks again for coming and helping us out with this."

"No problem. You know I'm happy to do it. I'll talk to you soon."

"Okay. Take care."

The two men shook hands and Dr. Stephenson left. When Mr. Coviello found himself alone in his classroom, he pulled out the compass case from his pocket. Taking a long hard look at the object, he thought, *I have my work cut out for me.*

Chapter 16

"IT FALLS BETWEEN THE FIFTEENTH and sixteenth centuries Shawn! Can you believe it?" Brandon asked Shawn as they walked home from school.

"No B. It's incredible!"

"I know. And I can't believe *I'm* the one who found it! I never have *any* luck finding things. Remember when I lost my watch in the pool last summer? I *still* haven't found it! Oh man!"

"That's right. It wasn't a very big pool either." The two boys laughed as they continued to walk.

"Hey Shawn, how many artifacts from the fifteenth and sixteenth centuries do you think even exist today?"

"I don't know B. You should have asked Dr. Stephenson."

"Yeah you're right. I guess I should have."

"Why do you want to know that anyway?"

"Because ... the more *rare* something is, the more *valuable* it is."

"Oh yeah, that's right. But don't forget what Mr. C and Dr. Stephenson said, Brandon. We still don't have all of the facts about the compass case. We don't even know who this thing belonged to."

"I know, I know. Hey, wasn't Dr. Stephenson a really cool guy? He must be a great teacher."

"Yep. But I still can't believe he never played in the NBA. Did you see how tall he was? Man, I hope *I* get to be that tall. I'd play center for the Knicks!"

"Wouldn't you rather play for the Yankees?"

"Hmmm. Tough choice. I guess I'll have to think about it."

Brandon rolled his eyes and continued to chat with his best pal as they made their way home. The boys had learned something very valuable about the compass case today.

Little did they know they would learn more sooner than they expected.

Chapter 17

A FEW DAYS LATER, MR. Coviello sat at the computer in his classroom, hoping to find whatever link he could to the letters engraved on the back of the compass. Ever since he disproved the "My Fire" message that was connected to St. Elmo, decoding the letters had become an obsession to him. He *had* to find something. It was just so difficult. He tried researching the symbolism of certain letters and their connection to navigation and exploration in the fifteenth and sixteenth centuries, but he came up with nothing. He tried to find any kind of significance that could be connected to the alignment of the letters, but to no avail. He even tried adding letters to the ones that could be read on the compass to determine what might have been scratched off, but the possibilities were endless. Frustration had officially set in, and he had no idea where to go next.

After blankly staring at the wall behind his computer monitor for what seemed like several minutes, Mr. Coviello thought, *There's something there John. You're just not seeing it. It's there.*

He looked at the compass case again. Perhaps, he decided, he should take a whole new approach to his research. Looking at the letters themselves had gotten him nowhere. What he needed to do was go *beyond* the letters and use the information that he had. Dr. Stephenson and his staff at the university had determined that the compass was from the fifteenth or sixteenth century. That was basically all they had so far. But maybe it was enough to help him find out what was engraved on the back of that case. What if, he thought, he made a list of all the navigators and explorers from that time period and researched each one? It would take quite some time, true, but it seemed like the most logical way to go.

Carefully and efficiently Mr. Coviello began to compile his list. It was an honor roll of famous explorers. As he clicked through several Web sites on his computer, he wrote down famous names such as Vasco Nunez de Balboa, John Cabot, Ferdinand Magellan, Amerigo Vespucci, Francisco Coronado, Juan Ponce de Leon, and of course Christopher Columbus. There were more to follow.

, Mr. C thought, *It's like a list of great heavyweight boxing champions. Who do I start with first?*

It was a very good question. He could begin by putting the explorers in chronological order according to the dates of their expeditions. He could also just list the names in alphabetical order and begin from there. *No*, he thought. That would bore him to death. Mr. Coviello knew that he wanted to begin with the "big fish," the one that got away when he and Dr. Stephenson had connected him to St. Elmo's fire. Yes. He wanted to begin with the most famous explorer of all. He wrote the name Christopher Columbus on the top of his list.

Okay Mr. Admiral of the Ocean Seas, Mr. C thought, _Let's see if you have anything to do with this compass._

Mr. Coviello went right to the search engine on his computer and began to type in key words along with Columbus's name. First he typed the words "symbols" and "Columbus" to see if any of the letters on the compass case could be linked to him. He found nothing. Next he entered the words "coat of arms" and "Columbus" into his search. Perhaps there was something there that could help him. When the links for his search came up, he clicked on one to see what the image looked like. The four quarters of the shield contained four symbolic pictures: a castle, a lion, a group of islands, and five anchors. The images and their symbolism were quite interesting, but unfortunately they seemed to have no link to the letters engraved on the compass. Once again — nothing.

Hmmm. What else can I try? he thought. _Could the letters on the case spell Columbus's name in a different language?_ It was worth a try. Quickly he typed the key words into the search engine. Several links came up that listed Columbus's name in many different languages. Mr. C chose one and carefully scanned the list of names. He saw the ones familiar to him written in English, Spanish, Italian, and Portuguese.

Christopher Columbus
Cristobal Colon
Cristoforo Colombo
Cristovao Colombo

He then began to look at the languages he was not very familiar with, such as Greek, Hebrew, and Russian.

Χριστόφορος Κολόμβος

סובמולוק רפוטסירכ

Христофор Колумб

The possibility of the letter X in the Greek and Russian names leading to something began to excite him, but the excitement quickly faded once he realized the names were too long and did not match the other existing letters. This wasn't what he was looking for. None of the other names worked either. He was 0 for 3.

Mr. Coviello was ready to pack up and head home after what had been a very long day when one more possibility for a search entered his head. How did Columbus identify himself in writing? Did he have a special signature? Did he use special symbols? It was a long shot, but it was worth a try. Mr. Coviello entered the words "Columbus" and "signature" into the search engine of his computer. Surprisingly, he found several links listed from his search. He found one that seemed to contain the information he needed, and began to scroll down. An image appeared halfway through the page. Mr. Coviello suddenly became short of breath.

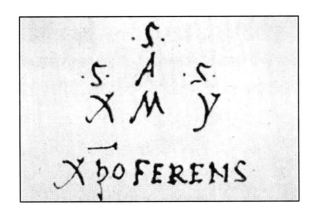

"Oh my God," he said quietly. He heard himself repeat the phrase several times before he came to his senses. When he did, he quickly pulled the compass case from his pocket and held it up to the computer screen. The alignment of the existing letters engraved on the case was a perfect match to Columbus's signature.

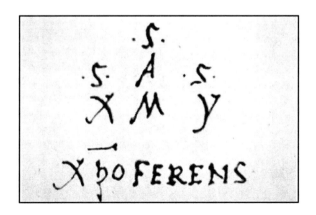

He had done it! The mystery of the engraving had been unlocked, and this time there was no disproving it. It was then that the ultimate possibility struck him. Could this compass actually have belonged to Christopher Columbus? The thought made the compass rattle as his hand shook nervously. As the excitement grew within him, Mr. Coviello began to piece together the facts. He started at the beginning. When Brandon first showed the case to him, he had said that he found it while vacationing at Punta Cana in the Dominican Republic. Of course! The Dominican Republic is part of an island called Hispaniola, which was named by Columbus after he discovered it during his first voyage to the New World. *Could Columbus have lost the compass while navigating this island?* Next he considered the age that had been determined from the testing done by Dr. Stephenson. *The age of the compass certainly dictated that it could have been from Columbus's time.* Finally he considered the signature on the case. There was no doubt now that the engraving on the case was linked to Columbus. It all lined up. There was a strong possibility that his student had found the Holy Grail: a navigational instrument used by the great Christopher Columbus.

Chapter 18

JOHN COVIELLO COULDN'T HELP HIMSELF. He had to stay and learn more about the signature of Columbus. The thought of going home for the day completely left him. *Feed the hungry minds.* Right now his mind was *starving*. With a sense of intense curiosity, Mr. C studied the signature. It was a unique pyramid of dots and letters. *What does it actually mean?* he thought. To find the answer to his question, he scrolled back to the beginning of the webpage that he originally chose from the search engine and began to read.

He learned that Columbus began to use this signature the month after he returned from his first voyage. He used it on almost everything he signed until his death, even though he never really explained what the mysterious arrangement meant.

Mr. C thought to himself, *another mystery. Was it is with this guy?"*

He continued to read that there were at least eight possible explanations for what the signature meant. One of the simplest suggestions offered this translation:

Servus

Sum Altissimi Salvatoris

Xristus Maria Yosephus

Xristo-Ferens

"Servant I am the Most Exalted Savior; Christ, Mary, and Joseph; Christ-bearer."

Other suggestions stated the use of the letter S in the pyramid represented the Holy Trinity: *Sanctus, Sanctus, Sanctus* ("Holy, Holy, Holy"). As he read through additional translations from various scholars, he found that virtually all of them were directed to Columbus's deep religious devotion. And while the first three lines of the signature were the subject of much speculation and controversy, there was no doubt about what the last line meant. The word is a half Greek, half Latin formation of Columbus's first name. It emphasizes that *Christopher* literally means "Christ-bearer."

Christ-bearer, Mr. C thought. *It certainly makes sense. Columbus believed it was his mission not only to claim new lands for Spain, but also to bring Christianity across the seas to "uncivilized" inhabitants. Simply fascinating.*

As he looked at the clock on the wall, he found that he should have left work two hours ago. Oh boy, late again. If he moved quickly, he would probably make it home just in time for dinner. Of course his tardiness would require an explanation to his wife, but that was okay. It was worth it. The time he put in to conduct his research provided answers about the compass that went beyond his wildest dreams. As far as John Coviello saw it, this was the best time he ever spent after school.

Part 3

Loose Lips Sink Ships

Chapter 19

IT HAD BEEN TWO HOURS since Dr. Stephenson fell into a deep sleep in his reading chair when the phone rang. The amplified sound of the ringing pierced what had been a very calm silence in his apartment. Startled and confused, the groggy professor jumped up, causing the novel that had been resting on his chest to fall to the floor. He looked at the clock on his wall and saw that the time was only 9:15 p.m. How strange. It had seemed much later to him.

I must be getting old, he thought.

By the fourth ring, he had been able to rise from his chair and get to the phone before his voicemail picked up. Clearing his throat, he greeted his caller.

"Hello. Dr. Jonas Stephenson."

"I did it!" an elated voice replied on the other end.

"Did what? Who is this?" Dr. Stephenson replied.

"It's me Dr. J. It's John Coviello!"

"Oh John! How are you? A little late to be calling isn't it?"

"Doc, it's not even 9:30 yet. Listen, forget about the time. *I did it!* I found out what the engraving on the back of the compass is *and* who it's connected to. This is going to blow your mind!"

"Really? Well now I'm not so mad that you woke me from my beauty sleep. What did you find out?"

"What if I told you that the compass case I'm holding in my hand right now might have belonged to a famous explorer?"

"Haven't we been down this road before?" Dr. Stephenson asked.

"We sure have. But this time the road has no dead end. What I found out about the compass case is not a theory Dr. J. It's a fact."

"Well what exactly did you find out?"

"I found out that the engraving on the back of this object is actually a pyramid of letters that makes up the signature of the great Christopher Columbus!"

Waiting for a reply, John Coviello heard the sound of a quiet gasp followed by a long silence.

"Dr. J, are you there?" he asked.

"Uh yes, I'm here John. Are you sure?"

"Absolutely. When I compared the back of the case to the image of Columbus's signature, it was a perfect match. Everything aligns perfectly!"

"Amazing! Not only that you discovered what the engraving is, but how quickly you found it! Of all the possibilities that you could have researched, what was it that brought you to Columbus?"

"Nothing more than dumb luck really. In looking at the estimated age of the object that you and your staff concluded through your dating tests, I knew I had a big job in front of me. There were so many navigators and explorers to research. It was a simple case of wanting to start with the explorer at the top — the most famous and in my opinion, the most interesting. It just happened. It was almost like I was *meant* to find this."

"Maybe you were John. Maybe you were. My goodness! This is incredible. Have you told the boys yet?"

"No, you are the first person I've spoken to about it. I plan on telling the boys tomorrow at school. They're going to be very excited."

"I would think so." said Dr. Stephenson. He then paused and continued.

"John, I think you need to be very careful about what you tell those boys. It's true that we have a great deal to be excited about. We have an estimated age of the object and we now know who the engraving on the back is connected to. There's a possibility that all of this can lead to something big. I'd be lying if I said I wasn't excited myself. However, we still do not have any *conclusive proof* that this object actually belonged to Columbus. When the boys learn of what you found, it will be very easy for them to let their imaginations run wild and get carried away. This may create hysteria and put the boys in a difficult situation. I've seen it happen with adults. I think it's important that we tell them to keep things quiet until we come up with more answers."

"I agree with you completely Dr. J. The last thing I want is for those boys to get hurt. I'll do everything I can to protect them from that."

"I know you will John."

"Well I guess I better get going. I'm going to *try* and get some sleep tonight."

"Yeah, I was doing pretty well with that until *you* called!"

The two men laughed and then wished each other a good night. Mr. Coviello promised to keep Dr. Stephenson informed of any new developments with the case. Tomorrow was going to be a big day. He was going to tell Brandon and Shawn about what he had found.

Chapter 20

BRANDON MORELLI WAS USUALLY A very light sleeper. However, tonight would be different. On this particular evening, he had fallen into a very deep sleep and began to dream. He wasn't sure how or why, but he found himself standing on the beach at Punta Cana once again feeling a sense of panic and urgency. The compass case he had found while snorkeling there had become lost, and somehow he had to find it.

As he walked along the shore, people he had never seen before watched him look for his lost treasure and began to laugh at him. As he walked further, he began to see many of his classmates, and they began to laugh at him as well.

Why are they laughing at me? he wondered to himself.

The laughter became louder and louder. The crashing of the waves onto the shore became more aggressive. Desperately he dug his hands into the sand to find the compass case, and suddenly all of the people around him disappeared and he was alone. The water became calm and the sun began to set on the beach. Just at the moment when he thought he would never see his compass again, he felt the presence of someone behind him and slowly turned to see who it was. Walking toward Brandon was an older man with a very familiar face, a face he definitely knew but couldn't pinpoint at the moment.

"Who are you?" Brandon asked him.

The man stood there and said nothing, looking at him with a stern and determined face. He then continued walking toward Brandon and extended his arm toward him. There was something in his hand. Brandon reached toward him and opened his hand to take it. Very carefully the mysterious man put what appeared to be a small bundle of seaweed in Brandon's hand.

"What is this?" Brandon asked.

Once again the man said nothing. He motioned for Brandon to unravel it. Inside the bundle of seaweed, he was amazed to find his missing compass case!

Quickly Brandon looked into the strange yet familiar face of the man again. This time, he was greeted with a warm fatherly smile.

"Thank you," Brandon said.

He looked down at the compass again, and as he began to ask the man a question, he noticed the man had disappeared. It was then that Brandon awoke drenched with sweat and filled with confusion.

That was a strange dream, he thought. *I know that man from somewhere. Who was he?*

Unfortunately for Brandon, the answer to that question would not come that night. He looked at the clock on his night table. It was 2:35 a.m. He was still groggy and tired. After sinking his head back into his pillow, he fell back asleep within minutes. By morning, he would forget all about the dream.

Chapter 21

THE NEXT DAY AFTER SCHOOL, Mr. Coviello sat Brandon and Shawn down in his classroom and began to reveal what he had discovered about the engraving on the back of the compass case. He did so in a very simple manner. First he put an image of Columbus's signature that he printed out from his computer on the table.

"Do either of you have any idea what this is?" he asked.

"Looks like some kind of code or something," said Brandon.

"Close Brandon. But not exactly."

Mr. C then put the compass case on the table next to the image of the signature. He gave the boys a few moments to look at them.

"Whoa!" Shawn exclaimed. "Is that what's engraved on there?"

"Yes it is Shawn. But the best part is yet to come. I'm going to tell you what this says and who it's connected to. Hold your breath boys."

With that, he began to explain that the pyramid of letters was the signature of Christopher Columbus. He showed them how the letters from the computer image aligned perfectly with the letters that remained on the compass case. He also explained the history of the signature, as well as the translations that were offered by the scholars who studied it.

The revelation sent Brandon's head spinning. Brandon stared at the image with his mouth ajar, absolutely overwhelmed. He remained both motionless and expressionless. Shawn's reaction was the total opposite. He couldn't physically contain himself. He began jumping up and down, throwing his arms into the air, and laughing hysterically.

"Okay fellas. Now that you have been brought up-to-date, I think we have some very important things to talk about," said Mr. C. "We have some very exciting possibilities in front of us here. The compass case Brandon found might be something very special."

"*Might* be?" Shawn asked. "Didn't you just find out that it *is* something special?"

"No Shawn, I didn't. And that's what I want to make clear to the two of you. As it stands right now, the compass case *might* have belonged to Christopher Columbus, but we do not have any conclusive proof that gives us 100 percent certainty. That being said, I think it would be a good idea to keep all of this to ourselves for now until we find out more. Does that make sense to you?"

"Can we tell our parents?" Brandon asked. "My mom and dad really want to know what's going on with the compass."

"Of course you can. As a matter of fact, I'm going to give your parents a call when I'm done speaking to the two of you. Now listen, outside of myself, the two of you, Dr. Stephenson, and your parents, no one else needs to know about the compass at this time. Believe me, it's for the best."

"Okay Mr. C," Brandon said. "I understand. I just have one question. When do I get my compass back?"

Mr. Coviello began to laugh. "Very soon Brandon. Very soon. Part of the reason why I'm calling your parents is to ask them for permission to hold it a while longer so that Dr. Stephenson can have another look at it. Don't worry. I'm not going to run away with it. This is *your* compass Brandon. You found it and you own it. As a matter of fact, if you don't feel comfortable with me holding it longer, I'll give it back to you right now."

"Oh no Mr. C, that's okay. I want Dr. Stephenson to see it again. Maybe the two of you can find out even more about it. Keep it."

"Okay, thanks. It won't be too much longer, I promise. Now I've had enough for today. Get lost you two. Go home, get some rest, and celebrate … *quietly.* I'll see you tomorrow."

"Thanks Mr. C! See you tomorrow!" Brandon said.

"Yeah, see you tomorrow Mr. C," added Shawn.

Mr. Coviello looked down at the old compass case in his hand. He smiled and pumped his fist in the air.

Chapter 22

"CHRISTOPHER COLUMBUS? WOW! THAT'S AMAZING Brandon!" Mrs. Morelli said after her son shared the big news at the dinner table.

"It certainly is," Mr. Morelli added. "I just can't believe it. Punta Cana is a resort area. I never would have thought in a million years that someone would find a historical artifact in the waters down there ... especially my son! This is great! I might be able to retire early after all!"

"Take it easy Dad. We haven't struck it rich yet. Mr. C said we still don't have any proof that the compass case even *belonged* to Columbus anyway."

"I know Son. I was just kidding about my retirement," Mr. Morelli said.

"What do you mean *you know*?"

"Well I didn't even tell your mother this yet, but I spoke to Mr. Coviello on the phone this afternoon. He told me everything that's been happening with the compass."

"Oh that's right. He said he was going to call you. Did he ask for permission to hold onto it a little while longer?"

"As a matter of fact he did. You know, Brandon, you're very lucky to have a guy like Mr. C as your teacher. He's a very nice man. While we were talking, he told me what a fine student you are. Apparently you remind him a lot of himself when he was your age."

"He told you that?" Brandon asked incredulously.

"Yep. That man thinks very highly of you Son."

This brought a giant smile to Brandon's face. To have someone like Mr. C pay him such a compliment was very flattering. His father continued.

"Mr. Coviello also told me that it would probably be a good idea to keep things low-key about the compass for a while. If you and Shawn were to go around telling all of your friends that you found Christopher Columbus's compass, it might put you guys in a difficult spot, especially since there's no proof right now that it belonged to him. Did he tell you that Brandon?"

"Yes he did."

"It's good advice. I'd listen to him if I were you."

"I will Dad. You know, in the beginning, I was really excited about the possibility being rich and famous. But now it's different. I don't think I even want people to know about it even if it turns out that it *did* belong to Columbus."

"You don't?" a shocked Mr. Morelli asked. "I don't think I understand Son."

"The compass case is mine Dad. For some reason *I* found it under those corals in Punta Cana. I'm not sure why it was me who found it, but I think there has to be some reason.

Anyway, if it turns out that this thing really did belong to Christopher Columbus, then a lot of people will want it. They will want to put it in a museum, or put it on television, or some other place where people will line up to see it. That's okay, and I understand why people would be so interested in it. But if that happens, it won't be _mine_ anymore. It will belong to _everybody_."

"Well if someone else had found this and it turned out to be something Columbus used or owned, wouldn't _you_ want to see it Brandon?" Mrs. Morelli asked.

"I know I sound selfish Mom, but somebody else didn't find it … I did! Ever since I brought it in to show Mr. C, I've felt a weird connection to it. There's something inside of me that's telling me to protect it and keep it for myself."

"Look Son, as you said, this object is _yours_. You know your mother and I will support whatever it is that will make you happy. If keeping it for yourself feels like the right thing to do, then do it. I just think you should take some time and think about all of the options that might be presented to you if it turns out this artifact is something special. Someone might make you an offer that you can't refuse."

"I know it sounds crazy Dad, but I don't care about being famous, and I don't care about being rich. Even if it turns out that Columbus had nothing to do with this thing, I don't care. It's special to me, and I'd like to keep it. Can I be excused please?"

Mr. and Mrs. Morelli looked at each other. Finally Mrs. Morelli excused her son.

"Yes, of course, honey."

Brandon offered a half-smile toward his parents and proceeded to go upstairs to his bedroom. He closed the door behind him.

"I never knew that old compass meant so much to him," a concerned Mrs. Morelli said to her husband.

"No, I guess I didn't either. You know how passionate he can get about things. If he says he wants to keep it, he means it."

"Yes he does. I just don't want him to get hurt over this Bob."

"I know honey. I don't want him to get hurt either."

"It's just that this whole thing could put a lot of pressure on him."

"Listen, don't worry. Our son is a smart boy. No matter what happens, I'm sure he'll do the right thing. I guess the best-case scenario is that the compass turns out to have no proven connection to Columbus. This way there won't be any pressure put on Brandon to do something he may not want to do. He can just keep the thing and be done with it."

"What if the compass turns out to be something more than we thought Bob?"

Mr. Morelli took a moment to think and then looked at his wife.

"Then we have to protect our son the same way he wants to protect that compass."

Chapter 23

THE NEXT MORNING, BRANDON WAS getting dressed for school when he heard a knock on his bedroom door. Slowly the door opened. It was his father.

"Good morning Son. You okay?" he asked.

"Yeah Dad. I'm fine. I was thinking about everything before I went to bed last night. Maybe I'm overreacting about being so protective of the compass case. I mean, if this thing really did belong to Columbus, other people should get to see it."

"That's *your* decision Son. You know that no matter what happens, your mother and I love you."

Mr. Morelli walked over to his son, kissed his head, and embraced him.

"We're very proud of you Brandon."

"Thanks Dad."

"Well I'm off to work. Have a good day at school, and I'll see you later."

"Okay, see you later. Love you Dad."

'I love you too, kid. Take care."

Brandon closed the door and continued getting ready for school. As he got dressed, he thought of how lucky he was to have such a great man as his father. He had always felt very close to him and loved him dearly. He knew that no matter how hard things became, he could always depend on his father to be there for him. Perhaps this is what made Brandon Morelli such a confident and capable young man.

After devouring a bowl of his favorite cereal and brushing his teeth, Brandon grabbed his lunch bag and read his mother's note next to it; she had left for work earlier that morning. The note read simply: *Have a great day honey. You are MY treasure!* The message brought a smile to his face.

"Love you too, Mom," he said softly.

Quickly he grabbed his books and made his way out of the house. He could hear the bus coming up the block, and he didn't want to miss it.

The bus picked up Brandon at the corner of his street, which he had sprinted to at full speed. When he got onto the bus, he noticed that Shawn was not aboard. That was strange. If Shawn was sick, he certainly would have known about it. Maybe he was running really late today. No matter. Brandon was sure he would see his buddy pop into school sometime this morning. When the bus pulled into the school parking lot ten minutes later, Shawn was there waiting for Brandon.

"Hey what are you doing here already?"

"I'm waiting for *you* B. I woke up early this morning, so I figured I'd come to school early. I ran here."

"You ran??? Shawn, school is about three miles away from our neighborhood."

"Yeah I know. I just felt like I had a lot of energy today."

"If you ran three miles to school, you must have had a *ton* of energy. C'mon, let's go to our lockers and get ready for class."

The two boys entered the halls of Eisenhower Middle School for what appeared to be another routine day. However, *this* day would turn out to be anything but routine. As soon as they reached their lockers, they were surrounded by their classmates. It was as if two celebrities had just come to their school to visit. Everyone seemed to immediately swarm around Brandon. Startled and confused, he found himself bombarded with questions about the compass case.

"Hey Brandon, is it true? Did you find Christopher Columbus's compass?"

"Yeah Brandon, where is it? Can I see it?"

"Has anyone offered you any money for it yet? You're gonna be rich!"

"Where is it now Brandon?"

"I don't believe it. How do you know it's real?"

The questions kept coming, and the hysteria became greater until Brandon tuned everything out of his head and looked over at Shawn. He didn't even have to ask his best friend how all of these kids knew about the compass. The answer was obvious. His best friend (or the person he *thought* was his best friend) had spilled the beans. A furious Brandon took Shawn by the arm and pulled him aside to confront him.

"Shawn, what have you done? You weren't supposed to tell *anyone* about this!"

"I know, I know. But Brandon, I couldn't help it. It's too exciting!"

"Mr. Coviello said it would be dangerous if we told anyone yet. We're not even a 100 percent sure that this thing is what you've *told* everyone it is! What if it doesn't turn out to be Columbus's compass?"

"C'mon B, you're overreacting. Everything's cool. Everyone wants to know about this. Right now you and I are the most popular kids in school. We might as well enjoy it, right?"

"Shawn, you're an idiot! I don't want to be the most popular kid in school, and I don't want everyone knowing about the compass case! This was our secret. You promised that you wouldn't tell anyone! You totally betrayed me!"

"*Betrayed* you? Oh come on, you've got to be kidding me. I thought you would like being *the man* at school. Look at this. You're a celebrity!"

"I don't feel like a celebrity; I feel like a fool! I was a fool to trust you, and I was a fool to think that you were really my friend. All you really care about is yourself!"

"Oh yeah? What about you? Ever since you showed that stupid compass to Mr. C you've been obsessed with it. It's like everything else around you just disappeared, and all you care about is finding out more about it. You think that just because you found that old thing it makes you special. Well you're not! You're just like everyone else!"

"I know I'm just like everyone else! The only difference is that *I* found the case. That means that *I* decide what is going to happen with it! You know, come to think of it, you really have nothing to do with this whole thing. _You_ didn't find it. It doesn't even _belong_ to you. And if I do make any money with this compass, I'm not giving you a cent! You don't deserve it!"

"That's fine with me sucker! I bet that the case is nothing but a fake anyway!"

"The only thing that's a _fake_ around here is you!"

"Whatever. I'm outta here. Have a nice life."

"Yeah. Whatever, Shawn."

With that, Shawn stormed off. After collecting himself, Brandon went back to his locker to retrieve his books for class. Having witnessed the heated exchange between the two boys, the other kids had scattered off and went about their business. As far as Brandon was concerned though, the damage had been done. The secret was out, and his friendship with Shawn was over. The day got off to a terrible start, and it seemed that things couldn't possibly get any worse.

When Brandon and Shawn came to social studies class at the beginning of fourth period, Mr. Coviello immediately sensed that something was wrong. It started when the boys entered his class separately. This was highly unusual, since they always came to class together. As a matter of fact, they came to _every_ class together.

Hmmm, Mr. C thought, _something's up_.

His hunch was confirmed by the demeanor of the two boys. They walked into his room looking as though someone had ripped the energy right out of them. Each one lethargically took his seat and then slumped into the chair, staring at the desk in front of him. Mr. C thought about making a joke to pep up things but decided it probably wasn't a good idea. The boys looked like they were in no mood for humor.

Well, he thought, *if they want to talk, I'm sure they'll come to me when they're ready. Better get on with the lesson.*

And so Mr. Coviello went on with his lesson about Colonial America and acted as if he didn't notice anything unusual about the boys' behavior. Brandon sat through the entire lesson unfocused, his mind spinning wildly. He wanted to pay attention to what Mr. C was saying, but he just couldn't. Things were getting totally out of control for him. He quickly glanced behind him to see what Shawn was doing; his former friend was staring into oblivion.

I can't believe he did this to me, Brandon thought. *After everything we've been through ... I can't believe he betrayed me!*

At the end of class, Shawn quickly collected his books and hurried into the hallway. His best friend had already exploded on him because he couldn't keep the secret; he didn't need Mr. C taking *his* turn. He had had enough of that for today. Meanwhile, Brandon waited for an opportunity to talk to his favorite teacher. Mr. Coviello was sitting patiently at his desk, while the students filed out of his classroom. Without any prompting from Brandon, Mr. C began the inevitable conversation.

"So what's going on between you and Shawn, Brandon?"

"Our friendship is over Mr. C," Brandon replied.

"Over? That sounds pretty extreme. Something big must have happened."

"It was something big all right. Shawn betrayed me Mr. C! In fact, he betrayed you too! He told everyone about the compass case! Everyone knows now! As soon as I came to school this morning, everyone was all over me asking me questions about it. It was terrible! I can't believe he did this!"

Mr. Coviello took a moment to absorb what had happened. He took a deep breath and then addressed his student.

"Brandon, I understand why you are upset. You have every right to be. We specifically told Shawn not to say anything, and he did anyway. That was wrong. However, is that really worth ending a friendship over? I mean, the two of you are like brothers, and sometimes even brothers have bad disagreements. Maybe you guys just need a few days to let things cool down and then you can patch things up."

"I don't want to patch things up with him. He's a traitor Mr. C! How can you be friends with a traitor? Being popular with the rest of the kids in school was more important to him than our friendship. He didn't care about me, and he didn't care about the compass case. It's over! I'm done with him!"

"I see you've got the classic Italian temper, kid. And I know what you are feeling. I've got a pretty bad one myself. When people cross you or betray you, you just want to cut them off and never acknowledge them again. It's almost like you make them disappear. I've felt like this many times in my life. But that can be very destructive Brandon, especially when it involves someone you care about. Good friendships and relationships are very important and very valuable. They're also hard to come by. If you're lucky enough to have a good friendship with someone, you should do everything you can to hold onto it because once it's lost, you may never find one like it again."

"I know. You're right Mr. C. I just can't help the way I feel right now. I'm so mad at him."

"I can see that, and you're right. We can't help the way we feel. Emotions are hard to control sometimes. But did you ever hear the expression 'time heals all wounds'? Give it some time Brandon. Think about the big picture. Is ending your friendship with Shawn something you really want?"

"No, but what about the compass Mr. C? He let out the secret. I won't even be able to walk to the bus without being harassed now."

"I know. It's not the end of the world though. Just try to play it off the best you can and tell them that it's probably nothing. Tell them Shawn overreacted a bit. Things will calm down. Now you better get going. You're going to be late for your next class."

"Okay. Thanks Mr. C. I'll see you tomorrow."

"See you tomorrow Brandon. Don't forget what I told you."

"I won't. I'll give it some time!"

"Good man."

With that, Brandon zipped down the hallway to his next class. Meanwhile Mr. Coviello paced around his desk in the empty classroom. He knew that Shawn had made a big mistake by revealing the secret of the compass, but he couldn't tell Brandon that. *Things are going to get a little crazy now*, he thought. He just hoped things wouldn't get *too* crazy.

Chapter 24

MR. COVIELLO HAD A FEELING that today was going to be eventful. The buzz about the compass case was all over the school now and had surely spilled over into the town of Monroe Park as well. Students, staff members, and townspeople would all want to know about it, and Brandon Morelli would be their primary source. This was a tremendous concern for Mr. C. Surely the twelve-year-old boy would not be able to handle the pressure and the stress of all the attention that was about to be paid to him. A boy like Brandon, although strong-minded, could easily break under those conditions. Almost any kid would. That was why he had told the boys to keep things quiet. He knew that if the secret got out, this is what would happen. It was not a good situation.

Well, he thought, *What's done is done. But I'll do whatever I have to in order to protect that kid.*

Mr. Coviello swore this vow to himself. Brandon was special to him. He was a gifted and talented young man.

What's more, he was a good kid who came from a nice family. There was no way he would let him get hurt.

He reached into his pocket and pulled out the compass case. Nobody knew that he still had it except for Brandon and his family, Shawn, and Dr. Stephenson. That was good, he thought, though he hoped that when Shawn let the secret out he didn't say anything about who had it. He would soon find out.

The school day had begun, and Mr. C prepared for his first-period class to come in. He knew he wouldn't see Brandon and Shawn until eighth period for their social studies class. Perhaps he could get his mind off of the situation and just concentrate on his teaching until this afternoon, he thought. *No chance.* As soon as his seventh-grade students entered his room, they flocked to his desk.

"We heard about the compass case Mr. C."

"Do you really have it?"

"Yeah, can we see it?"

"Is it locked in your desk?"

"Did it really belong to Christopher Columbus?"

Mr. Coviello wasn't left to wonder for very long if Shawn revealed who was holding the case. He obviously told the kids *everything.* Mr. C suddenly felt the burst of anger that Brandon must have felt when he first learned that Shawn had betrayed him.

"Everyone take your seats *right now!*" he said loudly and sternly.

The students quickly gathered themselves and made their way to their desks. The kids knew very well that Mr. C was a nice guy, but he was the type of guy you didn't want to see angry. Right now he was clearly angry. As soon as everyone was seated, there was complete silence. Their teacher began to address them.

"I don't know what it is that all of you have heard out in those hallways, but let me assure you that there seems to be a great deal of speculation and exaggeration going on. The rumors that are flying around this school, and this town for that matter, are just that: *rumors*. Someone in this school has decided to embellish the truth about a particular situation."

"Well isn't it true that one of your sixth-grade students found an old compass in the ocean when he was snorkeling in the Dominican Republic, Mr. C?" a girl in the front of the room asked.

There was no use in attempting to totally deny the whole situation. It was only a matter of time before everything surfaced anyway. So Mr. Coviello decided to tell his students just what they needed to know.

"Yes Nancy, that is true. One of my sixth-grade students found a compass case in the waters down there while he was vacationing. He thought I would be interested in it so he brought it in for me to see. There were some interesting markings on the object that I wanted to research, so I held onto the case for a few days. I came up with a few theories about what those markings might be, but the truth is, I haven't really come up with anything conclusive."

"Is it true that those markings are really Christopher Columbus's name and that it used to belong to him?" an eager student asked.

All eyes in the classroom widened.

"All I can tell you, Jimmy, is that it could be anything. But before anyone gets too excited, let me make very clear that unless you have clear-cut *proof* that it belonged to Columbus or anyone else, you really have nothing. Right now we have no conclusive proof that it belonged to Christopher Columbus. And even if those markings turn out to be Columbus's name, it doesn't mean the object actually belonged to him. Remember, people have been trying to make a buck since the beginning of time. Don't doubt for a second that false relics and artifacts were created by people hoping to make a profit by deceiving others. It's a problem that archaeologists have dealt with on many occasions. It may very well be that this particular object is a false artifact. Consider that to be your first crash-course in archaeology, ladies and gentlemen."

Mr. Coviello's comments seemed to calm the excitement in his classroom. He was pleased with the way he had handled the situation. However, he knew that he would probably have to give the same speech to the rest of his classes and other curious minds that he encountered throughout the course of his day. Now that he had temporarily diffused the hysteria, it was back to business.

"All right ladies and gentlemen. Let's get back to the business at hand. Everyone open your textbooks to page 303 and let's continue our discussion from yesterday." The students complied with their teacher's wishes and the class was back to normal.

The same could not be said for Brandon Morelli, though. His day was anything but normal. Countless students had approached him about the object, and countless times he had to explain that the rumors were exaggerations. Most of the curiosity about the compass was harmless, until he began receiving threats of bodily harm from some of the older students unless he showed it to them. It was at this point that Brandon realized what Mr. C had meant about this becoming a "dangerous" situation.

"Are you kidding me?" Brandon thought to himself.

The thought that anyone would actually threaten him over the compass totally baffled him. It made absolutely no sense. Then another realization suddenly came over him. If it was going to be this bad in *school*, what would it be like in the *outside world*? Would adults begin to harass him? Would his family be harassed? Would he and his family be safe? The answers to these questions really scared him.

"Hey Brandon!" a voice called from behind in the hallway. It was his friend Jimmy from the baseball team.

"What's up Jimmy?" Brandon said cautiously.

"I heard that Mr. Coviello has that compass that everyone is talking about in his room. Is that true?"

Brandon froze for a second. He didn't know what to say. How did Jimmy know that Mr. C had the compass case? Did Shawn tell everyone that too? Apparently he did. Brandon thought very carefully about the answer he was about to give. If he lied and told Jimmy that it wasn't true and then the truth eventually surfaced, anything he said in the future about the rumors regarding the compass case would have no credibility. People would think that he was covering something up. It was a safer play to tell the truth.

"Yeah it's true Jimmy. I gave it to him to hold because I wanted him to look at it. He knows a lot of stuff about archaeology and I wanted to see if he could find out something about it."

"Didn't he find out that it belonged to Columbus? That's what Shawn said."

"No that's not what he found out. I don't know why Shawn is telling everyone that, but it's not true. If you don't believe me, you can ask Mr. C."

"No I believe you Brandon. But why is Shawn going around telling everyone that you found a famous artifact?"

"I think he likes the attention."

"Yeah I guess so. I'll see you later Brandon."

"See you later Jimmy."

It was now clear that everyone knew Mr. Coviello was holding the case. In a strange way this gave Brandon some comfort. He knew that Mr. C was probably going through the same type of interrogations from the kids as he did. He also knew that Mr. C would do everything he possibly could to diffuse the situation. That was a relief to Brandon. He was not in this alone anymore, and he had his hero as his ally: The Great Mr. C.

Chapter 25

EIGHTH PERIOD HAD COME. IT was time for Mr. Coviello's social studies class, and Shawn Thompson felt sick to his stomach as he stood inside a stall in the boys' bathroom. Breaking into a cold sweat, he thought about everything that had happened in the last two days. He had told practically the whole school community about Brandon's compass case in order to catapult his status among his peers. The hopes of fame and popularity had driven him to reveal a secret he had promised to keep.

When he began to tell everyone yesterday, it was great. Dozens of kids approached him to hear the story of the compass. He was the center of attention, and it was the greatest feeling in the world. But then something happened that he didn't expect. Brandon became furious at him. In fact, his best friend felt so betrayed by what he had done that he completely swore him out of his life. That wasn't what Shawn wanted.

Why didn't Brandon understand? he wondered. *I was just trying to do something good for the both of us.*

In addition to losing his best friend, he now couldn't even face his favorite teacher anymore. Mr. C had told him not to say anything, and he *completely* disregarded him. How could he ever walk into that classroom again without feeling silly and embarrassed? Mr. C probably hated him now, just like Brandon did. Shawn started to realize that the price for what he had done was more than he could bear.

I'm a sell-out, he thought. *I sold out my friend, I sold out my teacher, and … I sold out myself.*

He slowly opened the door to the stall and walked over to the sink. He looked at himself in the mirror and quickly realized that he didn't like what he saw. Suddenly the late bell rang for eighth-period classes. Shawn was late for Mr. C's class, but it didn't matter.

I'll face Mr. Coviello and Brandon soon enough, he thought, *but not today.*

With that, he decided to go to the nurse's office and skip social studies. Since he already looked ill from the tremendous amount of stress he felt, getting out of eighth period would not be a tough sell. He walked into the empty hallway and found that he was alone. It was the worst feeling in the world.

Chapter 26

BRANDON ARRIVED AT MR. COVIELLO'S room just as the late bell rang. He had been doing this in all his other classes to avoid any barrage of questions from his classmates. It was a strategy that proved to be very effective, though he hated having to avoid everyone. Once again a burst of anger began to flare up at Shawn, who had put him in this awkward position.

Just forget it, he thought in an attempt to calm down. Strangely it was his *parents'* voices he heard giving him advice.

What's done is done, Brandon. Getting angry won't change what happened. Concentrate on Mr. C's lesson and then you can talk to him after school.

It was good advice, and he was amazed how the influence of his mother and father permeated through his thoughts at that moment.

On entering the room, Brandon saw something very unusual. None of the students were in their seats. They were all crowded around Mr. C's desk, shifting and peering in to get a better look at something. Even stranger, there were several adults in the room who appeared to have Mr. C surrounded behind his desk, asking questions and taking pictures with their cameras. Faculty members and students from other classes came down the hallways and were now making their way into the room as well. It was chaos!

What in the world is going on here? Brandon wondered.

He would soon find out. One of the students in the crowd suddenly noticed that Brandon had just entered the room and exclaimed, "It's Brandon!"

Within seconds, the crowd of students and adults descended on him. A jolt of fear shot through his entire body.

Immediately the strange adults in the room, who were obviously reporters, began throwing questions at him.

"Brandon Morelli? Lance Wilson, Channel 9 News. Can you tell us how you found the compass that some believe was once owned by the great Christopher Columbus?"

Brandon didn't know what to do. Should he answer the question? Should he just keep quiet? What was going on here? As he tried to make sense of the situation, microphones were being pushed toward his face. Camera flashbulbs were popping in front of him, causing temporary blindness. Reporters from the local papers were scribbling notes on their pads. Suddenly another question came.

"Brandon, can you tell us what exactly the engraving on the compass case said?"

Once again Brandon froze with indecision, simply looking around for a way out of this. There didn't appear to be one.

The fact that Brandon had not answered any questions yet did not deter the reporters from asking more.

"Brandon, how do we know that this whole thing isn't a hoax? Is it true that this is just a prank to get some cheap publicity? Do you really expect us to believe that you found a compass that was used by Christopher Columbus??? C'mon, kid, give us the real story here."

The reporter who asked this question was a large man with an intimidating disposition. Brandon wasn't prepared to be bullied like that. Suddenly he felt a large lump in his throat and tears begin to well up in his eyes. He was about to completely break down when he heard a volcanic eruption. It was the voice of his savior.

"That's enough!!! Get away from that boy right now!!!"

In an instant all of the madness stopped, and everyone turned to see who had issued the loud, sharp command. It was Mr. Coviello, who was accompanied by the school principal, Mr. Torres. Mr. C had a look about him that Brandon had never seen before. He looked like a man possessed with anger who was about to go to war. With Mr. Torres following behind him, Mr. C marched through the crowd of people in his room. The two men parted the crowd like the Red Sea. Mr. Coviello pushed the microphones out of Brandon's face and placed his hands on his student's shoulders in a protective gesture. Brandon looked up at Mr. C with tears streaming down his face.

"It's okay Brandon. It's over," Mr. C said as he took Brandon's head into his chest. "This whole thing ends right now."

Mr. Torres, who was a large man with a deep voice and a commanding presence, began to address the reporters in the crowd.

"I don't know how you people found your way into this building, but let me assure you that the police are on their way now to help you find your way out! This is a school. It is an institution of learning for our children. It's my job to make sure those children feel safe and secure while they learn, and I will not have even one of them being cornered and intimidated by people who don't belong here."

Mr. Coviello walked up behind Mr. Torres and put his hand on his shoulder to indicate that he had something to say. Mr. Torres took a step back and gave the floor to Mr. C. Everyone remained quiet to hear him speak.

"All of you are here today because you want a story. You want to make the big headline for your newspapers, or you want to be very first channel to bring people an exclusive report. I understand that because it's what you do. It's your job. However, I believe part of your job is to act responsibly. You came here today because of the rumors that have been floating around this school and this town about this young boy and the compass case he found. You barged into my classroom when I was just about to teach a lesson and you bombarded me with questions. You jammed cameras and microphones in my face. You had no regard for me or my students. You had to have your story. Even though you don't belong here and you made your way into the building under what I'm sure were false pretenses, what you did to me was okay because I'm an adult and I can handle it. But then you stepped over the line. You cornered a young boy who was only expecting to come to his social studies class to learn about colonial life and totally blindsided him. You cornered him. You intimidated him. You invaded what was once a safe place for him. Worst of all, you broke this kid down. Is that responsible? Is that something you can be proud of? Do you people even care about what you just did to this kid? Let me clue you in on a little secret, *we have no conclusive proof that the compass case Brandon found had anything to do with Christopher Columbus!* None at all! What you've just done may have caused damage to that young boy that cannot be fixed. And for what? For this?"

Mr. Coviello made his way over to his desk to retrieve the compass case where he had left it. Suddenly he froze. The case wasn't there! Mr. C began to panic. He scanned the top of his desk. He looked through all of his desk drawers. He checked the floor around his desk. He checked his pockets. It was nowhere to be found.

"John, what's wrong? Is everything all right?" Mr. Torres asked.

"No, everything's not all right. The compass case is gone! Someone must have taken it from my desk!"

A large gasp came over the room as everyone began to look at each other in disbelief. Someone had actually taken the compass from Mr. C's desk! Who would dare do something like that? Was it a student? Was it one of the reporters? There was really no way to tell with all of the people who had been in and out of the room.

"All right," Mr. Torres said, "that's it. Everyone out! I want all teachers and students to return to their classes, and everyone else out of the building! I am notifying the police of what occurred here today when they arrive."

With that, the room began to empty quickly. As he glared at each person walking out, Brandon began to wonder if he was staring at the person who took his compass. He desperately wanted to confront and interrogate each one until he found the guilty party. Sadly though, he couldn't. The shock of the unexpected interviews from the reporters left him physically and emotionally drained. He felt so helpless, small, and weak. Would he have felt much different if a bully had beaten him up and taken his compass? *Probably not*, he thought. Fighting his emotions to the best of his ability, Brandon tried once again to hold back the tears that were building up in his eyes, but it was no use. He broke down again. Embarrassed and ashamed, he buried his head in his arms and slumped to the floor.

Mr. Coviello saw Brandon from the other side of the room, and his heart sank. His student had just endured a terrible and traumatic experience. He knew that the disappearance of the compass would be a huge blow to Brandon, and he feared that it might be a blow from which he would never recover.

That poor kid put so much of himself into that compass, he thought as he walked toward Brandon. *So much of his hopes and dreams were linked to it.*

Someone had taken it. Just like that it was gone. How could it have come to this? Mr. C looked terrible. Perhaps he felt that he had failed Brandon because *he* was the one who left the compass on his desk. Would Brandon lash out at him? Would he say that he wished he never showed it to him? Maybe he would say nothing at all and just walk out on him. Mr. C hoped that none of these scenarios would take place as he began to sit beside his student on the floor.

"Brandon, I'm so sorry," he began. "I'm so sorry I lost your compass. You put your trust in me and I failed you. I can't tell you enough how badly I feel about this."

Brandon's head rose quickly and he immediately wiped the tears from his face. He looked at Mr. C with a serious, perplexed expression. He then began to shake his head to dismiss what his teacher had just said.

"No, Mr. C. I won't accept your apology," he began. Mr. C's heart began to sink with regret. Brandon then continued.

"I won't accept your apology because you didn't do anything wrong. You didn't lose the compass case, Mr. C. Someone took it. Someone *stole* it. It's not your fault."

"That may be true Brandon, but I feel responsible. When you came into my class room and I saw the crowd of reporters begin to swarm you, I had to do something quickly. I immediately ran out and headed straight to Mr. Torres's office to inform him what was going on because I knew he would call the police and get those people out of the building. In my haste, I must have left the compass on my desk. During the few minutes I was gone, anyone could have taken it. How could I have been so foolish? I guess everything happened so fast, I didn't have time to think. I'm really sorry Brandon. Never in a million years did I think this could happen."

"It's okay Mr. C. You did what you did because you were trying to help me. I don't know how much longer I could have taken those reporters if you hadn't shown up. Man, you really scared the daylights out of everyone too. I never knew you could yell like that."

"Well when I saw what those people were doing to you and I saw the look on your face, I guess I just lost it. I don't want anyone messing with one of my kids."

"Thanks Mr. C."

"No problem Brandon. And I want you to know that this isn't the end of all of this. Mr. Torres and I are going to have the police conduct a full investigation of what happened here today. We won't give up until we find your compass case."

"Okay. I sure hope we get it back. We still have a lot of work to do with it."

Mr. C smiled. "You bet we do, and I intend to finish it. Now listen, you've had a rough day. Mr. Torres and I would like you to go to the office and sit for a while. We're going to call your parents, inform them of what happened, and have them take you home. It's probably best for you to be with your family right now."

"That's true. Well I guess I'll get going. Thanks again for helping me Mr. C."

"You're very welcome Brandon. And remember what I told you. We're not going to give up until we find that compass!"

Brandon smiled at his teacher, but deep inside he had a feeling that he would never see his compass again.

Chapter 27

MRS. MORELLI HAD COME AS quickly as possible to pick up her son from school. Having heard from Mr. Torres about everything that had transpired, she was deeply concerned for Brandon. She knew how much that compass case meant to him and how devastated he must feel right now. As she walked into the school's main office, she found Brandon sitting there with Mr. Torres. He looked like he had just run a marathon. She quickly walked over to him and gently took his face into her hands.

"Honey are you okay?" she asked.

"Yeah Mom, I'm fine, but someone took the compass."

"I know, Brandon. Mr. Torres told me about everything on the phone. I'm so sorry about what happened."

"Me too," Brandon said dejectedly.

"Brandon's had a rough day Mrs. Morelli," Mr. Torres said. "He endured quite a bit. But I want to tell you how proud I am of the way he handled himself."

Brandon was incredulous. "How can you be proud of me Mr. Torres? I broke down. I cried."

"I'm proud of you because you handled yourself like a gentleman with those reporters, Brandon. You could have been rude to them if you wanted to, but you weren't. You could have yelled and acted wildly, but you didn't. You handled yourself with class young man. That says a lot about you, and it says a lot about the job your parents have done with you."

Brandon and his mother smiled. They were both very flattered. Mr. Torres continued.

"And let me tell you something else. Just because you cried, it doesn't mean you are weak, and it doesn't mean you are not a man. You were put in a situation today that was very trying emotionally. You simply reacted to the way you felt. People like to think that they can always control their emotions, but they can't. It's part of being human. You hold your head high Son."

"Thanks Mr. Torres," Brandon said. "I will."

"Mr. Torres, I want to thank you so much for what you did for my son today," Mrs. Morelli said. "This school is very lucky to have you."

"It was my pleasure Mrs. Morelli. And thank you for the compliment."

"See you later Mr. Torres," Brandon said.

"See you later Brandon."

Brandon took a few steps toward the door when Mr. Torres stopped him.

"Brandon, you *will* get that compass case back. I won't give up, and I don't want *you* to give up."

"I won't Mr. Torres. Bye."

"Bye-bye."

The car ride home from school was very quiet. Brandon didn't feel like talking very much, and Mrs. Morelli decided it was a good idea to give her son some quiet time to collect himself. When they pulled into their driveway, Mr. Morelli was sitting on the front steps waiting for them. He still had his suit on from work and had obviously come home early. Brandon was surprised to see him.

"Mom, what is Dad doing home so early?" he asked.

"On my way to pick you up from school, I called him and told him what happened. He insisted on coming home. He's very worried about you."

Brandon smiled. He knew his father would always be there for him. When he stepped out of the car, his father approached him immediately and embraced him.

"Are you okay Son?" Mr. Morelli asked.

"I'm okay Dad. I just had a long day."

"I know you did. Let's go inside and you can relax."

On entering the house, Mr. Morelli noticed how exhausted his son looked.

"You look very tired Brandon. Maybe it would be a good idea if you went upstairs and took a nap. We can talk about what happened today after you've charged your battery a bit, okay?"

"Okay Dad. That's probably a good idea."

Brandon slowly made his way up the stairs and into his room. His bed became the most welcome sight of the day. He collapsed onto it and fell into a very deep sleep. Five minutes later, Mr. Morelli peeked into Brandon's room to check on him. His son was out like a light.

"Get some rest Son," he whispered to Brandon. He quietly stepped out and closed the door behind him.

When Brandon awoke from his nap, he looked out the windows of his room and saw that it was dark out. How long had he been sleeping? He checked the clock on his night table and saw that it was 6 p.m. He had been asleep for two and a half hours.

Boy, I guess I was really tired, he thought.

Still groggy and weak from his much-needed slumber, Brandon decided to head downstairs to be with his parents. It was just about dinnertime, and he could hear his stomach begin to growl. Eating a good meal always made him feel better, no matter how bad things seemed.

As he began to make his way down the stairs, he heard the voices of his parents engaged in a conversation with someone. Did his parents plan on having company tonight? Why hadn't they told him about it? When he reached the bottom of the stairs, he quickly found out who his parents were talking to.

"What is *he* doing here?" Brandon angrily asked his parents.

Sitting on the living room couch opposite his mother and father was his former best friend, Shawn Thompson.

"Shawn came to talk to us Brandon … and to you too," Mr. Morelli informed him.

"There's nothing to talk about," he said sharply.

"Now wait just a second," his father began sternly. "It took a lot of courage for Shawn to come here tonight. I think the least you can do is hear him out. Your mother and I have been talking with Shawn for the last twenty minutes, and we think you might be interested in what he has to say."

"Fine," Brandon said curtly. "Whatever."

"The two of you can sit right here and talk," Mrs. Morelli said. "Your father and I will go to the kitchen so you can have some privacy."

With that, Brandon's parents left the room. For a few seconds, there was complete silence. Brandon kept his gaze fixed on the floor in front of him. He refused to make eye contact with Shawn. Finally Shawn began the conversation.

"How you doing B?" he asked nervously.

Brandon offered no answer, which was just the reaction that Shawn expected. Determined to get his feelings off his chest, Shawn continued.

"Look Brandon, I know you hate me. I know you don't want to be my friend anymore. I know that you really want nothing to do with me too. I just wanted to come here tonight to tell you a few things, and then I'll leave. Okay?"

Brandon continued to stare at the floor with an expressionless face. He gave no physical gestures to acknowledge that he had heard what Shawn just said.

"Here it goes," Shawn said as he prepared to bear his soul to the boy who had been like a brother to him for most of his life.

"For the past couple of days, I've had the chance to think about what I've done. Telling everybody about the compass case belonging to Christopher Columbus was really stupid Brandon. I didn't think so at the time, because I thought I was doing something cool for the both of us, but it was. You were right; I betrayed you. You trusted me to keep a secret and I didn't. I took that secret and I used it for myself. I should have realized that our friendship was more important than being the most popular kid in school. Like I said, it was stupid. Things really backfired on me too. Everyone in school thinks I'm a liar and a jerk. I can't face my favorite teacher anymore because I lied to him, and worst of all, I lost my best friend. I've got nothing now Brandon. I really messed up."

Brandon looked up at Shawn for the first time and noticed that his former friend looked terrible. It looked like he hadn't eaten or had much sleep for the past two days. He really looked beaten down. Now it was Shawn staring at the floor as he continued to talk to Brandon.

"You know, I heard about what happened in Mr. C's class today. I heard how those reporters and all of those kids cornered you and asked you all of those questions. I'm so sorry about that Brandon. If it wasn't for me and my big mouth, none of that would have happened. Your mom and dad also told me that someone took the compass. That's my fault too. This whole thing is my fault, which is why I understand if you want nothing to do with me. I don't blame you man. If someone did this to me, I'd feel the same way."

Shawn began to get up and walk toward the door, but then turned to face Brandon.

"I just want you to know Brandon, that I never ever wanted you to get hurt. Even if we never say another word to each other again, it's important to me that you know that. That's all I wanted to say. See you later."

Brandon felt the stone wall he had built around his heart begin to crumble. It was obvious that Shawn had suffered as much from his foolish mistake as he had, maybe even more. Was it really necessary to make him suffer more by continuing to shut him out of his life? No it wasn't. Living without the compass case was going to be tough, but living without his best friend would be worse.

"Hey," Brandon called out. Shawn turned with a look of surprise.

"The last time we you were here, you whipped me in the video home run derby. You owe me a rematch."

"Okay," Shawn said, fighting back overwhelming feelings of emotion. "You got it."

Both boys walked toward each other with smiles from ear to ear. They then locked hands in their customary handshake. The fight was over, and the dream team was back together. Brandon heard everything he needed to hear from Shawn, and no other words about the incident were necessary. Somehow both boys understood this.

"C'mon," Brandon said to Shawn, "we'll play best of three—like we always do."

"Cool," Shawn replied. "But don't get mad when I whip you again."

The two boys raced upstairs into Brandon's room. After the flurry of footsteps subsided, Mr. and Mrs. Morelli emerged from the kitchen smiling and hugging each other.

"Well that worked out pretty well don't you think?" Mr. Morelli asked his wife.

"Yes it did," she responded. "Oh Bob, I'm so happy they're friends again. Those two really need each other, especially now."

"Yeah I know. It was only a matter of time before those two would patch things up. I'm glad it was sooner rather than later. I'm going to call Shawn's mom and tell her that he's probably going to be staying for dinner. I'm sure she won't mind given the circumstances."

"Okay. I'll tell the boys that we're eating in five minutes."

The reconciliation between Brandon and Shawn was a huge relief for Mr. and Mrs. Morelli. After the day their son had endured, anything positive that happened was very welcome.

Chapter 28

"I CAN'T DO IT B," Shawn said to Brandon with a knot in his stomach. "I don't think I can face him."

"Yes you can Shawn. You had the courage to face me and my parents last night, and you can do this too."

"I know. I'm just really nervous that's all."

"Weren't you nervous last night too?"

"Yes."

"Well this is no different. Just go up to him and tell him what's on your mind. It will be fine. Hey, you're going to have to do it sooner or later, right? You might as well do it now. Go ahead. I'll wait for you right outside the door."

"Okay B. Here goes nothing."

Shawn nervously walked into Mr. Coviello's classroom. It was only eight o'clock in the morning, and classes would not begin for another twenty-five minutes. Mr. C. was sitting at his desk grading papers when he saw Shawn walk in.

"Hello Shawn." Mr. C said, pretending to be more surprised than he actually was.

"Hi Mr. C. I was wondering if I could talk to you for a minute."

"Of course you can. Pull up a chair."

"Thanks," Shawn said as he sat in a desk right in front of Mr. C's. Taking a deep breath, he began to address his teacher.

"Mr. C, I wanted to apologize to you for everything that's happened in the last couple of days. I know that I caused you and Brandon a lot of trouble because of my big mouth, and I'm really sorry. You told us to keep things quiet about the compass case, and I didn't listen. I guess I let my excitement get the better of me. I should have listened to what you said."

Mr. Coviello nodded slowly to acknowledge what Shawn had said. He rose from his seat, walked around his desk, and stood right in front him.

"Yes you should have listened Shawn. What you did was very foolish and irresponsible. It caused quite a bit of craziness around here, and it caused some people to be put in a very difficult situation. However, I accept your apology. It took courage to come in here and apologize, and I appreciate that. I also think that you learned a valuable lesson from all of this, don't you?"

"Yes Mr. C. I learned that you should listen to people who know what they're talking about."

"What else did you learn?"

Shawn thought for a moment. "I learned that sometimes what you say can cause a lot of people to get hurt. You should think before you say something stupid."

Mr. C smiled. "That's right my friend. You've got it. I'm glad you understand that. Now have you spoken to Brandon yet?"

"Yep, he has," a voice from outside the door said.

"I should have known," Mr. C said laughing. "Get in here Brandon!"

Brandon emerged with a big smile on his face and entered the room. He pulled up a desk next to Shawn and sat down.

"Well it's nice to see that the old gang is back together," Mr. C said. "However, it doesn't mean that it's the end of our problems here. Take a look at this."

Mr. C took the local newspaper from his desk and opened it. Once he found the page he was looking for, he folded the paper in half and set it on the desk in front of the boys. Brandon read the headline:

Compass Possibly Linked to Columbus Feared Stolen

"Go ahead," Mr. C said, "read the whole article."

Together, the boys read the article carefully and intensely. Brandon, in particular, was completely fixated by what he read. When he finally finished reading, he was furious.

"I don't believe it," he said. "They didn't even put my name in this! They just say the compass was found by _a boy in the sixth grade._"

"That may not be such a bad thing," Mr. C said. "The last thing you want is more attention from the press, right?"

"That's true," Brandon said. "But look at this. They left so much out. They didn't talk about how they barged into the school when they weren't supposed to be here, they didn't talk about how they interrupted your class, and they didn't talk about how they terrorized me!"

"Did you really think the press would say those things about themselves Brandon? There's no way. All they care about is getting a story. How they go about getting it is a nonissue to them. Welcome to the world of the media gentlemen."

"That's messed up," Shawn said. "What jerks!"

"Yeah," Brandon said, "but here's the part that's *really* messed up. They said that they are offering a *cash reward* to anyone who has information about the whereabouts of the compass. That's ridiculous! How can they offer a reward for something that doesn't even belong to them?"

"I wouldn't worry about that too much Brandon. First of all, it's been well-established that *you* are the rightful owner of the compass. Second, I think the reason they are offering a reward is so *they* can be the first ones to break the news if it's found. Believe me, they'd like nothing better than to have a picture of you and the editor of their newspaper on the front page shaking hands as he gives the compass back to you."

"So this is all about them breaking another story?" Brandon asked.

"You got it," Mr. C said.

"Well as long as I get my compass back, I don't care *who* gets credit for it. The trouble is I don't think I'm ever going to see it again."

"I disagree," Mr. C said sternly. "I have a very strong feeling you're going to get it back ... maybe even sooner than you think."

"How can you know that Mr. C?" Shawn asked. Brandon nodded his head as if to show that his friend had taken the words right out of his mouth.

"Because I'm keeping a positive attitude boys, and I refuse to give up. It's been *one day* since this happened. You have to give it some time. Somehow, someway, this object will be returned to you. Listen to me boys. I want you to stay positive, and I don't want you to lose hope. Do you understand me?"

Both boys nodded and answered together, "Yes Mr. C."

"Good. You know if I hear anything, I'll contact you immediately. Until then, we just have to be patient and carry on with our lives. I know it's going to be difficult, but we really have no other choice. Now it's almost time for classes to begin. You two better get going."

"Okay Mr. C," Brandon said. "See you in social studies class."

"Later Mr. C," Shawn said. "Thank you."

"Sure," Mr. C replied. "See you later."

The boys walked together to their lockers to retrieve their books for class. As they walked, many of their peers began to stare at them and whisper to one another. Were they shocked that the two boys were friends again? Were they still talking about the stolen compass? It didn't matter. Brandon and Shawn had been through a lot in the past couple of days, so they simply dismissed it. As they were in the process of gathering their books for their first class, one of their buddies from the baseball team approached them. It was Jimmy.

"Hey guys, what's up?" he asked.

"Oh. Hey Jimmy," Brandon said after turning to see who it was.

"What's up Jimmy?" Shawn said cautiously.

"Nothing really. I'm just surprised to see you two together. I thought you guys weren't talking to each other."

Brandon and Shawn looked at each other and smiled. It became clear now why the other kids were staring. They too must have shared in Jimmy's surprise, but just didn't have the courage to ask about it.

"That's all over now," Shawn said.

"Yep," Brandon added. "We talked about everything that happened, and we just want to forget about it now."

"That's cool," Jimmy said. "I didn't think you two would stay mad at each other for long anyway. Hey are you guys going to the batting cages today?"

"We might," Brandon said.

"Okay. Maybe I'll see you guys there. See ya later."

"Later Jimmy." The boys said.

"I guess we're going to have to deal with funny looks for the next couple of days," Brandon said as the boys walked to class.

"That's okay," Shawn said. "It won't last that long. Like Mr. C said, we just have to give it some time."

"That's true. I don't care anyway. I'm just ignoring them."

"Yeah, me too. C'mon, we're going to be late if we don't get going."

Together the boys entered class and sat down in their seats. It appeared that Mr. C was right. Getting back to normal was going to be difficult. However, the boys seemed to be on their way. They had taken the first step.

Chapter 29

WHEN THE SCHOOL DAY ENDED, Brandon and Shawn slowly boarded the bus and sat in their usual spots on the way home. It had been a very busy day, and they were both exhausted. The rest of the day didn't promise to be any easier either, with the amount of homework and studying they had in front of them. But somehow the heavy workload was fine with the two boys. It would serve as a distraction to everything that was happening around them concerning the lost compass. As these thoughts roamed through their heads, there was very little discussion between the two. They sat quietly and enjoyed the ride.

Once the bus reached their stop, Brandon and Shawn grabbed their backpacks and stepped off. There would be no fake sparring or foot races today. The boys had an unspoken understanding that a straight, easy stroll was the approach they would take. As they turned the corner from the bus stop, Brandon spotted a small group of people waiting in his driveway.

"Who is that in my driveway?" he asked with a panic.

"I don't know," Shawn said. "Let's get closer and find out."

The boys picked up their pace and headed straight to Brandon's house. One of the people in the driveway spotted the boys and began to point, specifically at Brandon.

"There he is!" a woman shouted.

"Oh no," Brandon groaned.

"What? What is it?" Shawn asked.

"Those people are reporters Shawn. They're probably here to ask me about the compass case being stolen. I can't believe this!"

Brandon felt a sense of fear as he did the last time he encountered these reporters, but this time he didn't feel all alone. His best friend was with him now. This made him feel a lot better.

"This is your house B. If you don't want them here, tell them to get lost."

"I *don't* want them here, and that's exactly what I plan to do!"

As Brandon walked up his driveway, the questioning from the reporters began.

"Brandon? Brandon Morelli? Would you mind answering a few questions?"

The reporters didn't wait for an answer.

"Who do you think took the compass Brandon?"

"Why did you leave it with your teacher to hold if it belonged to you?"

"If the compass is found, do you plan to give it to a museum? Will you sell it?"

Brandon could feel the blood in his body begin to boil. He wanted no part of this, especially at his own house. For the first time, he was going to say something to them.

"I'm not answering any questions!" he said forcefully. "You people don't belong here. Please leave!"

"C'mon Brandon," one reporter said. "We just want a few statements and then we'll go. Give us something here."

"I'll give you something fool," Shawn said with attitude as he made his stand next to his best pal. "My friend said he's not answering any questions. He wants you to leave. So get lost!"

Just then a car quickly pulled into the driveway. It was Brandon's father. He quickly parked and nearly jumped out of the vehicle. Once out, he headed straight for the reporters.

"Would you people tell me why you're in my driveway bothering my son?"

"Mr. Morelli, we're with the—

"I don't care *who* you're with," Mr. Morelli shouted angrily. "Pack yourselves up and get out of here before I call the police. This is private property!"

The group of reporters gathered their things and began to leave. Brandon and Shawn looked at each other and smiled.

"One more thing," Brandon's father said aggressively. "Stay away from my son!"

Mr. Morelli stood at the bottom of his driveway refusing to budge until the reporters drove out of sight. Soon they were gone.

"Okay fellas," he said, "I don't think you have to worry about *that* happening again. Let's go inside and get some ice cream. Sound like a plan?"

"Sure," Brandon said.

"What about you Shawn?" Mr. Morelli asked.

"I'm always up for ice cream," he replied.

"Good. Let's go."

About ten minutes later, Mrs. Morelli entered the kitchen to find her husband and the two boys going to town on a half-gallon of mint chocolate chip.

"Did someone forget to tell me about the big afternoon snack?" she asked. "Bob, what are you doing home so early?"

"Things were a little slow at the office today, honey, so I decided to come home early. Turns out it was a good thing I did."

"Why? What happened?" she asked.

"Brandon and Shawn had some unexpected visitors waiting in our driveway as they were coming home from school."

"Who? Don't tell me it was more of those reporters."

"You guessed it."

"That's it, I've had it! This is getting to be absolutely ridiculous! What is wrong with those people?"

"Don't worry about it, dear, I took care of it."

"You took care of it?"

"Yep."

"Yeah," Brandon said, "Dad let 'em have it."

"That's right," Shawn chimed in. "Those fools took off faster than you could spell P-O-L-I-C-E."

Everyone began to laugh at Shawn's observation. It lightened what was a very tense situation at the moment.

"Well," Mrs. Morelli said, "if that's the case, get me a bowl. I could go for a little mint chocolate chip myself."

When everyone was finished eating their ice cream, Shawn announced that he had to get home.

"Are you sure you don't want to stay for dinner Shawn?" Brandon's mother asked.

"No thank you Mrs. Morelli. I've got a lot of homework to do tonight and a quiz to study for. Maybe some other time."

"Okay honey. Tell your mom we all said hello."

"I will. See you later."

Brandon walked with Shawn on his way to the door. Together they went outside.

"Hey Shawn," Brandon said.

"What's up?" Shawn asked.

"I just want to thank you for standing up for me with those reporters before. It made a big difference today knowing that I had you with me."

"No problem B. I wasn't going to let those turkeys bother you again. They had a lot of nerve waiting here in your driveway like that. Who do those fools think they are?"

"I don't know. I'm just glad it's over."

"Yeah, me too. Well listen, I really better get going if I'm going to finish all of this homework. I'll see you tomorrow."

"Okay Shawn. See you tomorrow."

Just as Brandon was about to close the door behind him to go inside, he heard Shawn yell from the corner.

"Hey Brandon! We got through another day! Things will get better! We just have to give it some time, man!"

Brandon smiled, waved to Shawn, and closed the door behind him. His best friend was right. Things were tough now, but time *would* heal all wounds.

Chapter 30

AFTER A FEW WEEKS, IT seemed that all of the madness had come to a stop. Things at school were pretty much back to normal, there were no more reporters bothering Brandon for a story, and he and Shawn had never been tighter. It was almost as if the whole incident with the lost compass case never existed. This was a relief to Brandon, but it also filled him with a sense of despair. Had it all been a dream? Did the compass case that bore the signature of Christopher Columbus ever really belong to him? The "calming of the storm" gave Brandon time to reflect. As his mind crossed the boundaries between fantasy and reality, the answers soon became painfully clear. It wasn't all a dream. Everything he remembered had certainly happened. He had found that magical object during his summer vacation. He had shared an incredible journey of research with his favorite teacher, which resulted in an amazing discovery. He had somehow made a deep emotional connection with the most famous explorer in history. And then it suddenly ended. Everything came to a screeching halt when the compass was taken from him. Why? Why did it all have to end? The empty hole in his heart that began to heal with the passage of time started to open again. The result was a feeling of terrible pain, and knowing that he was helpless to do anything about it made the pain even worse.

I've got to stop this, he thought. *I've got to stop torturing myself and come to grips with reality. The compass is gone. It's gone. There's nothing I can do to change what happened. It's over. I've got to deal with it and just move on.*

Brandon had an inner strength that would allow him to deal with this situation. He knew it was there, and he knew that it would get him through this. He was a survivor and he was for the most part, an optimist. He called on the advice his mother had bestowed upon him many times:

"Brandon, as bad as things get, they will *always* get better."

The words gave him comfort. He trusted this wisdom that came from his mother and found that in his eleven years of life experience, it was indeed true. Things *would* get better.

The first sign of this promise came with the change of seasons. Spring had finally arrived after what had been a long difficult winter. It was the season of new beginnings, a time of rebirth. For Brandon it also meant something else ... baseball season was here! For this reason alone, he looked forward to spring more than any other season. If ever there was something that would get Brandon's mind off of the compass, it was baseball.

Brandon loved baseball to the point that he became truly lost in it. With a burst of enthusiasm, he reminded himself that it wouldn't be long before he set foot on the diamond again. Oh how his senses filled with delight! The smell of fresh-cut grass from the field and the scent of well-oiled leather gloves would only be paralleled by the all-too familiar sound the crack of the bat made when the ball was hit. There was nothing like it! As great as these things were, however, there was something about America's pastime that Brandon enjoyed more than anything else when he played, and that was putting on the uniform. There was something about putting on the uniform that made him feel special. All of his baseball heroes had their own uniforms that gave them their hero-like identities. They all looked so sharp, so official. They were the closest thing to real-life costumed superheroes that Brandon had ever seen. He loved the way they wore their hats, how the brims seemed to be curved perfectly over their faces. Whenever he received a new hat at the beginning of each season, he spent hours bending and holding the brim until he felt it was trained just like theirs. He also loved the jerseys they wore, how they seemed to be tucked in perfectly as they boldly displayed the team names across the front and the numbers on the back. He made sure that during the course of every game, his jersey was tucked in and neat. Getting the jersey dirty was always okay of course, because it showed you were playing the game hard. However, he always made sure that it was clean and ready to go for the next one. This sometimes became a difficult task for his mother, but she knew how much it meant to him. He deeply believed in the adage look like a pro, play like a pro.

As Brandon's mind fell deeper into the realm of baseball ecstasy, thoughts of his past troubles quickly disappeared. Spring surely was a time of new beginnings.

Part 4

A Successful Voyage

Chapter 31

"C'MON BRANDON! GET ME IN!" Shawn yelled on a beautiful May afternoon as he stood on second base. He had just drilled a line drive down the third base line for a double and represented the tying run in a 9-8 game. This was last licks for the Blue Knights, and if they didn't get it done here, the game was over. Knowing the difference between victory and defeat rested on his bat, Brandon Morelli stepped to the plate with two outs.

Brandon's parents watched nervously from the stands. Mrs. Morelli sat with her hands folded, pressed against her chin. Mr. Morelli stood from his seat in the bleachers with his arms folded tightly. Neither shouted any words of encouragement to their son. Rather, they both spoke softly, almost as if they were speaking to themselves.

"Okay Son," Mr. Morelli said. "Be patient. Wait for your pitch."

"C'mon honey," Mrs. Morelli said, "you can do it."

Brandon stepped to the plate and took a deep breath. Never had he come to bat in such a high-pressure situation, but he knew it was bound to happen sooner or later. Every kid who plays baseball fantasizes about getting the winning hit in a big game, but very few realize how stressful it is to be put in a situation where all eyes are on you. Brandon became aware of this very quickly, but reminded himself that all he needed to concentrate on was the ball. *See the ball. See the ball. Block everything else out. See the ball.*

Brandon dug his feet into the batter's box and began to take his half-swings as he stared into the eyes of the Cardinals' pitcher. He was a tall, lanky boy whose long blonde hair shot out from under his cap. He threw pretty hard for a kid his age and proved to be an imposing figure on the mound. Before Shawn had hit his double, the hard-throwing hurler had struck out the previous two batters. Surely he had the same plan in mind for Brandon. He carefully looked in at the catcher for his sign and prepared to deliver his first pitch. It was a hard fastball that was outside of the plate.

"Ball!" the umpire yelled.

"That's it Brandon, wait for your pitch!" his coach yelled from the dugout.

"Good eye B!" Shawn yelled from second base.

The count was 1-0. Brandon took a deep breath and prepared for the next pitch. The pitcher wound up and delivered. This time he was more accurate and fired a fastball right down the middle.

"Strike one!"

Wow, Brandon thought. *That was fast!*

For the first time since he stepped to the plate, he felt hints of doubt enter his mind. This guy threw hard! _What if he couldn't catch up to these pitches?_

"No!" a voice shouted in his head. "Don't think like that! No fear! If this guy throws hard, you've got to swing hard. There's too much on the line!"

He dug his feet in a little deeper and lowered his brow to show that he meant business. This was a showdown, and he wasn't going to be intimidated. The Cardinals' pitcher quickly received his next sign and began to deliver. Zip! It was another fastball that sailed right into Brandon's hitting zone. With a good hard swing, he put the bat on the ball. Crack! The line drive zipped over the third baseman's head but landed just wide of the foul line.

"Foul ball!" the umpire yelled from behind the plate. "Foul ball!"

The spectators in the bleachers who were rooting for the Blue Knights let out a collective "Ohhhh" in disappointment.

"That's it B! You're on it now!" Shawn shouted. "Straighten it out!"

Mr. and Mrs. Morelli maintained their positions in the stands as if they were statues. This was almost too much to take. With two strikes on their son, they knew there was no room for error now. Both of them let out a deep breath as Brandon readied himself for the next pitch.

The opposing pitcher stood on the mound with the ball in his glove. He looked a lot more confident now, almost as if he could smell a strikeout coming. He was ahead in the count and knew that with one more good pitch this game would be over. Brandon took notice of his adversary's boost in confidence and it angered him.

He thinks he's got me, he thought, *but it's not over yet.*

As soon as the pitcher got his sign, he began his windup and delivered the pitch. When it came in, it looked as if it was going to hit Brandon, so he moved out of the way. The ball, however, started to curve and moved toward the plate. It just missed the inside corner.

"Ball!" the umpire called. "Inside!"

The Cardinals' pitcher threw his hands up in the air in disbelief. He thought the pitch was a strike. His coach apparently felt the same way.

"C'mon blue!" he said. ("Blue" is a term used by players and coaches to refer to an umpire, usually because umpires wear blue shirts.) "That was a strike! It hit the inside part of the plate!"

"It was inside Coach," the umpire responded.

Rather than engage the umpire in an argument, the Cardinals' coach waved him off and shouted more words of encouragement to his pitcher. The tension of this game had escalated to an even higher level now, with coaches, players, and spectators all cheering, clapping, and shouting words of encouragement.

Brandon stepped out of the batter's box and took another deep breath. He realized he had dodged a bullet with that last pitch. The curveball took him completely off -guard, and just missed the plate. The count was now 2-2. Before he stepped back into the box, Brandon thought about what pitch he was going to see next.

Think. If you were him, what would you throw next?

The answer was obvious and seemed to make perfect sense ... *another curveball*. It had frozen him the first time, and the pitcher was well-aware of it. It was his knockout pitch. He would most likely throw another one. There was, of course, a chance that he would throw a fastball instead, mixing things up and catching Brandon by surprise. What should he look for? Curveball or fastball? He had to decide. After a few seconds of indecision, he suddenly remembered how his father taught him that baseball sometimes turns into a guessing game where you have to lock into a decision and stay with it. It was then that he determined what his approach would be. He would look for the curveball.

"C'mon batter, let's go," the umpire said to him. "Play ball!"

Brandon stepped to the plate and tapped it twice with his bat. Once again he blocked out everything around him except for the pitcher. This was it ... the moment of truth. Everything could be decided by what this next pitch would be. If he guessed right, he had a chance to put the ball in play. If he guessed wrong, the game could be over. As these thoughts raced around in his head, the ball flew out of the pitcher's hand. Once again it headed toward Brandon, looking as if it would hit him. Then suddenly, the ball began to curve! He guessed right! Curveball! Brandon kept his weight down on his back leg and waited for the ball to break. This time the ball broke right in his hitting zone. With a tight grip and a strong swing, Brandon connected with the ball. Boom! The ball flew off of the barrel of the bat and soared into the air. The Cardinals' pitcher didn't bother to look at where it was going, he simply dropped his head in disappointment.

Brandon rounded first somewhere between a jog and a full sprint, watching the ball continue to fly. Back, back, back, the left fielder went. Suddenly he stopped and pounded his fist in his glove. Was he about to make the catch? Was the game going to end this way? The answer became clear to everyone when the outfielder abandoned his pursuit and turned back toward the field. The ball sailed well over his head and cleared the fence for a home run! He did it! The Blue Knights had won! Brandon felt as if he were walking on air as he rounded the bases and headed home. All of his teammates were jumping up and down waiting for him there, led by his best friend Shawn. As soon as he touched home plate, he was mobbed by his teammates. Up in the stands, Mr. and Mrs. Morelli were hugging each other as they jumped up and down. People were coming from all over congratulating them on what their son had just done.

"You did it B!" Shawn yelled to Brandon as the team celebrated at home plate. "You crushed it! Did you see how far that ball went?"

Brandon was beaming. "Yeah! I can't believe it! I never hit a ball like that before! This is awesome!"

The entire team and the coaches hoisted Brandon up on their shoulders and carried him off of the field. He was a hero. The feeling was like nothing he had ever experienced, and he would never forget it as long as he lived.

When the celebration on the field was over, Brandon saw his parents waiting for him. He quickly ran over to them, and they embraced in a group hug.

"Son that just qualified as one of the greatest moments of my life!" Mr. Morelli said. Brandon noticed that his father was teary-eyed. "I can't tell you enough how proud I am of you."

"Thanks Dad," Brandon said. "I still can't believe I did that."

"Well believe it honey," Mrs. Morelli said proudly. "You were absolutely great out there! You hit that ball so far!"

"Yeah I know! It's like a dream and I don't want to wake up!"

"Don't worry Son. This is no dream. You did it. Let's go home and celebrate!"

"Okay Dad. Let's go!"

The Morelli family proudly walked off the field. When they arrived home, Brandon's father announced that they would be going out to dinner at their favorite restaurant. It was a perfect day, and it seemed to Brandon that things couldn't possibly get any better than this.

Chapter 32

THE NEXT DAY BRANDON WOKE up with his face still beaming. He couldn't believe he had become a baseball hero by hitting that dramatic home run. Springing up from his bed, he went over to the mirror on his closet door and reenacted the swing that won the game for his team.

"Boom! There it goes! Going, Going, Gone!"

All night, he had replayed the magical moment in his mind, and not once did it get boring or old. How could it? It was the greatest moment of his life! He took another look at his reflection in the mirror and pumped his fist as if to say "Way to go!" Soon, however, Brandon decided that the time for self-glorification was over and the time for breakfast had come. He was hungry, and he knew that his parents would be waiting for him in the kitchen, still bubbling over with pride and excitement.

As expected, as soon as Brandon entered the kitchen he was quickly greeted by his parents, who were drinking their coffee at the table.

"There he is," his father said as if he were introducing a celebrity. "Ladies and gentlemen, Babe Ruth has entered the kitchen!"

Mr. and Mrs. Morelli both stood and applauded their son. Seizing the moment, Brandon once again reenacted the now-famous home-run swing and trotted around the kitchen table. His parents were delighted with the display and roared with laughter as they continued to clap. When Brandon's trot was finished, he went over to his parents and embraced each of them.

"Well," his mother asked him after the laughter had subsided, "what would Babe Ruth like for breakfast?

"Pancakes! You haven't made those in a long time Mom."

"All right," his mother said. "Pancakes it is. Pull up a chair and I'll have them ready in a few minutes."

Brandon quickly made himself comfortable at the table. It was always a special treat when his mother made pancakes, and he couldn't wait to tear into them. While his mother prepared the batter, Brandon's father folded up the newspaper he was reading and looked at his son as if he had something exciting to share.

"What? What is it Dad?" Brandon asked.

"Well, it seems that we are going to have some surprise visitors today," his father said with a smile.

"Really? Who?"

"Guess."

"Oh come on Dad! Just tell me! It could be anybody!"

"Okay, okay. Calm down. I'll tell you. Your grandmother and grandfather are flying in from Florida, and they're going to spend the week with us!"

"Grandma and Grandpa are coming? Yes! That's awesome! I really miss them!"

"They miss you too honey," his mother said. "They always say that they love living down in Florida, but the one thing they regret about it is that they don't get to see you as often as they would like. They're really excited about coming up to visit!"

"Not as excited as I am! I can't wait to tell them about the home run I hit yesterday!"

"Well before we do anything Son, we have to clean this house and get the guest room ready for your grandparents. Eat your pancakes, and when you're finished, go upstairs and straighten out your room. They should be here by noon."

"Okay Dad," Brandon said as his mother placed a tall stack of pancakes in front of him. "I just hope I can move after eating all of this!"

After Brandon devoured the pancakes in a manner that his mother described as a "feeding frenzy," he made his way up the stairs with a full belly and a sense of excitement.

I can't believe this, he thought, *I'm actually excited about cleaning my room! What's the world coming to?*

It wasn't every day that his grandparents made a special visit like this, so Brandon decided to put every effort into making his room look immaculate. He made his bed, picked all of the clothes off the floor, and even cleaned up his desk.

It actually looked nice! As he applied the finishing touches to his room, his mother walked in.

"My goodness," she said, "your room hasn't looked this neat in *years*!"

"Very funny Mom."

"Now that your room is clean, why don't you take a shower and get dressed for the day? Your father and I have some quick errands to run. We should be back by the time you finish."

"Okay. See you in a little while."

"See ya. We'll be back soon."

Thirty minutes later, Brandon was clean as a whistle and dressed nicely for the highly anticipated visit. As he came down the stairs, he heard the front door open. His parents were just returning from their errands.

"Good timing," his father said as he walked into the house. "Go outside and help your mother with the bags in the car. We picked up a few odds and ends."

Brandon knew what "odds and ends" meant: food! Whenever company was coming over, his parents always put out a great spread for their guests. Surely they had gone to the Italian deli and the bakery while they were out. Brandon ran outside to see if he was right.

"Honey can you take this in for me?" his mother asked as she held up a big white box with red and white string tied around it.

"Sure. What is it?"

Brandon knew what it was, but he needed confirmation.

"Cannoli! We bought a big box of them from the bakery!"

"Yes! I love cannoli!" he said.

"I know. Your grandparents do too."

Brandon took the box and ran inside while his mother brought in the bags from the deli. He placed the box on the kitchen table and went to the drawer to retrieve a pair of scissors to open it. Just when he was about to snip the string, his mother stopped him dead in his tracks.

"Hey! What do you think you're doing mister?"

"I was just going to make sure the cannoli were fresh for Grandma and Grandpa."

"What a noble gesture," she said sarcastically. "Put the scissors away."

Mr. Morelli suddenly stepped in to provide his son with some assistance.

"You know honey, I think Brandon might be right about this. I mean, what kind of hosts would we be if we served our guests cannoli that weren't fresh? Surely some sort of taste test is in order here."

Mrs. Morelli rolled her eyes and shook her head.

"You know, you're as bad as he is," she said to her husband. "I'm dealing with two crazed cannoli fanatics! Fine, the two of you can split one, but that's it! We're saving the rest for when Grandma and Grandpa come. Go ahead, conduct your taste test."

Brandon and his father looked at each other, smiled, and gave each other a high-five. Mission accomplished! They sat down at the table while Mrs. Morelli took a cannoli from the box and split it for the two of them. It was quickly established that the cannoli were indeed fresh. Taste test successful!

As Brandon and his father were finishing their snack, the doorbell rang, taking everyone by surprise.

"That's odd," Mrs. Morelli said. "I thought they weren't due to arrive for another couple of hours. Do you think they caught an earlier flight?"

"Maybe," Mr. Morelli said as he rose from his seat. "Brandon, why don't you get the door?"

"Sure!" Brandon said excitedly. He jumped up and ran to the door. As he moved across the living room, he thought about the big fuss his grandparents would make over how tall and how handsome he was. They always did that every time they saw him. He also thought about what they would bring him from Florida. There was never a time when his grandparents came without bearing gifts. With these thoughts dashing through his head, Brandon swung the door open and was about to say "Hi!" when he was quickly taken off guard. Waiting there on his porch were two people, but they weren't his grandparents. In fact, they were two people that Brandon would never expect to see at his home.

"Hello Brandon," one of them said. "I guess you're a little surprised to see us. May we come in?"

Speechless and confused, Brandon led the two men into his living room. Shortly after, his parents came in from the kitchen.

Brandon introduced the visitors.

"Mom, Dad, I'd like you to meet my teacher, Mr. Coviello, and his friend Dr. Stephenson."

Chapter 33

THE UNEXPECTED VISIT FROM MR. Coviello and Dr. Stephenson came way out of left field. It was a pleasant surprise for Brandon because he liked these two men a great deal, but it was a surprise nonetheless. He thought his parents' reaction to their visit would match his, but strangely, it didn't. As a matter of fact, his parents' behavior suggested that this visit was somehow expected.

"Mr. Coviello, it's a pleasure to finally meet you in person," Mr. Morelli said as he warmly shook hands with the teacher whom his son had always spoken highly of. He turned to the large gentleman and extended the same gesture.

"Dr. Stephenson, it's very nice to meet you. Welcome to our home."

"It's a pleasure Mr. Morelli," Dr. Stephenson said. "Thank you for having us here today."

Mrs. Morelli followed her husband and warmly greeted the two men.

"Welcome. Please make yourselves comfortable gentlemen. I'll be right back with some refreshments."

"Thank you Mrs. Morelli," Mr. Coviello said.

As Mr. Coviello and Dr. Stephenson settled into the large couch in the living room, Brandon's father motioned for him to take a seat as well. There was obviously a reason for this visit, and it clearly involved Brandon.

"Well," Mr. C began as he turned his attention to Brandon, "I suppose you're wondering why we are here today."

"Yeah, I am actually," Brandon said. "This is a big surprise."

"Yes and no," Mr. C said to his pupil.

"What do you mean Mr. C?"

"Brandon, Dr. Stephenson and I didn't come here by chance today. This was a visit that was in the making for several months now."

Brandon was totally lost. The look on his face had made this very clear.

"I don't understand Mr. C. What's going on? Am I in some kind of trouble?"

"No, no, no. Of course not. You're not in any kind of trouble at all. It's not *that* kind of visit. We're here today because we have something to share with you."

Suddenly Brandon's thoughts went right to the lost compass.

"Did they catch the guy who stole my compass? Is that what it is?"

"No Brandon, that's not it. It's actually something else."

Brandon's heart sunk with disappointment.

"Oh," he said dejectedly.

Dr. Stephenson saw the look of sadness on the young man's face and spoke up for the first time.

"Brandon, there's something very important that Mr. Coviello has to tell you. I think it's best that you sit back, relax, and let him explain why we're really here today."

"Okay Dr. Stephenson."

Just as Mr. Coviello was about to speak, Mrs. Morelli came into the room with a tray of refreshments and set it on the table in front of the men. Everyone helped themselves to a drink and a fresh cannoli.

"Thank you Mrs. Morelli," Mr. C said. "I love these things."

Mrs. Morelli smiled and said "You're very welcome."

It was then that Mr. C began to address Brandon.

"Before I tell you everything, I want you to understand that the people who are sitting in this room right now care about you very much and have your very best interests in mind. There is no one here that would ever do anything to harm you or hurt you. You really need to understand that."

Brandon's confusion only increased. "Okay," he said unsurely.

Mr. C continued. "Brandon, there are times in our lives when bad things happen to us. We don't always realize it, but sometimes these things aren't what they seem, and they actually turn out to be something good later on."

"You mean like my compass being stolen? I'm sorry Mr. C, but I can't see how any good could come out of that."

"Bear with me. You need to hear this whole thing out. There's a lot you don't know, and I'm here to fill you in. Listen carefully. A few months ago, I told you and Shawn to keep things quiet after I figured out that the engraving on the back of the compass was the signature of Columbus. I knew that if the word got out about this, you were going to have a lot of people giving you a hard time. Unfortunately that is exactly what came to pass. Brandon, I'm going to tell you what _really_ happened the day the compass was stolen."

What does he mean what really happened? Brandon wondered. Mr. C had already explained to him what happened the day that the compass was stolen. Did he leave something out?

"Mr. C, didn't you already tell me what happened? You told me that when you saw all of those reporters surrounding me in your classroom, you ran to get Mr. Torres. When the two of you came back to the room, the compass that you left on the desk was gone. Someone took it."

"Yes Brandon, that's what I _told_ you, and it's basically the truth ... but not all of it. There's more. You see, while Mr. Torres and I were making our way back to the classroom, I devised a plan to protect you and the compass. I knew that everyone was directing all of their attention toward you at the time, so I decided to use that to my advantage. Right before we entered the classroom, I gave Mr. Torres the compass case to hold for me. I explained to him what I planned to do, and he agreed to go along with it."

Brandon's eyes were as big as saucers now. He couldn't believe what he was hearing. Could it be true? He sat motionless and dared not move until Mr. C finished.

"There were so many people in my classroom when we returned that I knew when I claimed the compass was taken from my desk, everyone would be looking at each other to see who had it. It worked perfectly."

Mr. C could see something happening in Brandon's eyes. It was as if new life had been breathed into him. However, he could sense that Brandon still needed final confirmation. He needed to hear the words.

"That's right Brandon. Your compass was never stolen. No one even came close to it. The whole thing was staged."

"Y-You faked it? You faked that whole thing?" Brandon asked incredulously.

"Yes I did. I'm very sorry about all of the pain it caused you, but it was the best way I could think of to protect you. I knew how much that compass meant to you, and I knew those reporters would never leave you alone once they found out about it. Something had to be done. I figured that by making the compass disappear, I could make *them* disappear. I knew it would take a lot of time for the problem to go away completely, but it seems to have worked like a charm. My only regret about the whole thing was that I had to keep this a secret from you, and that you were hurt because of it."

"I can't believe it," Brandon said. He turned to his father. "Dad, did you and Mom know about this?"

"Yes Son, we did. Mr. Coviello called us the day after this happened and told us everything. We all agreed that keeping this a secret was in your best interests."

Brandon was in shock. *His parents knew about this the whole time and never said a word about it. Unbelievable! How could they do this? They saw how miserable he was without the compass.*

They knew how torn apart he would become every time he thought about it being stolen. He had suffered for months! How could they keep this from him? Brandon started to become angry.

"My own parents? My own mother and father knew all along that the compass was never stolen and you didn't tell me? I was miserable Dad! Was being miserable in my best interests?"

Before Mr. Morelli could answer his son, Mr. Coviello stood up and spoke.

"Brandon, you don't understand. Your mother and father *did* act in your best interests. They kept that secret to make sure that no one would bother or harass their son anymore. They were *protecting* you. I'm quite sure that it tore them apart to see you suffering when you thought the compass was stolen. But they knew your suffering would be temporary. It was your long-term well-being that was most important to them. They knew that when the time was right, the truth would be revealed to you and the compass would be returned to you. Think about it, Brandon."

Brandon knew that he had made a mistake. His parents didn't do anything wrong. They were just trying to protect their son. He felt awful for blowing up at his father.

"I'm sorry Dad. I didn't mean to get mad at you like that. I just didn't understand why you and Mom did what you did."

Mr. Morelli embraced his son.

"It's okay Brandon. You know that your mother and I would never do anything to hurt you. We love you very much."

"I know," Brandon said as he continued to hug his dad.

"Brandon," Mr. Morelli said to Brandon after their embrace, "I want you to know that Mr. C really stuck his neck out to make sure you were safe and that no one would try to take that compass case from you. He didn't have to do it, but he did."

Brandon walked over to Mr. C and shook his hand.

"Thank you Mr. C. Thanks for looking out for me."

"You're welcome Brandon. We Italians have to stick together, right?"

"Right! By the way, Mr. C, where is it? Where is the compass?

"Oh I'm sorry, but I don't have it. I gave it to someone to hold for me until it was time to return it to you."

"Who?" Brandon asked.

"Someone I trust. Someone who knows what to do in these situations."

The anticipation was getting the better of Brandon.

"Who?" he asked again almost laughing.

After a long pause, Dr. Stephenson rose to his feet and reached into his pocket, pulling out the compass.

"*Me,*" he said as he smiled and handed it to Brandon.

The moment he had desperately wanted for so long had finally come. Brandon was reunited with his lost compass case. Holding the compass in his hands once again was like magic, but before he could get too involved in this reunion, Brandon felt one of Dr. Stephenson's massive hands gently fall on his shoulder, calling attention to something he wanted to say. The giant gentleman began to address him.

"You know Brandon, the object you hold in your hands is very unique. There are so many questions that surround it, and those questions may never be answered. I had a great deal of time to conduct my own research on this compass case while it was in my possession. I tried to find something that would lead to a breakthrough in determining if this navigational instrument actually belonged to Christopher Columbus. Unfortunately, that breakthrough never happened. I used all of my skills and all of my resources. I consulted with colleagues I've worked with past and present. I even read through all of Columbus's journals _twice_ to see if there was any mention of such an object. Unfortunately there was nothing that provided any concrete proof that this belonged to him. Now I want to be very clear about something. All of this does not mean that this object _couldn't_ have belonged to him. It very well may have. Remember, the testing we conducted on the object dated it between the fifteenth and sixteenth centuries. You also have an engraving on the back of this case that looks to be the signature mark of Columbus himself. There's no doubt that these things offer intriguing possibilities. However, we'll probably never know for sure. And so, Brandon, the compass case becomes an object of faith. It will be whatever you believe it to be. Through my conversations with you, Mr. Coviello, and your parents, I've come to know what your beliefs are. You don't care about the money or the fame this compass might bring you. You only care about the happiness it brings you. _Always_ prosper in that happiness, young man. It's something that money can't always buy."

Dr. Stephenson extended his hand to Brandon.

"Thank you for allowing me to be a part of this adventure."

Brandon put out his hand and watched it disappear inside of Dr. Stephenson's as he shook it.

"Thank *you*, Dr. Stephenson. Thanks for all of your help. I really learned a lot from you."

"It was my pleasure Brandon," Dr. Stephenson said. He then turned to Mr. C.

"Well John, what do you say we get out of here and let these people enjoy the rest of their day?"

"Sounds like a good idea Doc."

The men got up from the couch and walked toward the door.

"Mr. Coviello, Dr. Stephenson, I just want to thank you for everything that you did for my son. My wife and I really appreciate it," Mr. Morelli said.

"You're welcome Mr. Morelli," Mr. C said. "Brandon is a great kid. I'm glad this whole thing worked out."

"Me too," Brandon said smiling.

"I'll see you tomorrow in class young scholar."

"See you tomorrow Mr. C."

"Take care of yourselves everyone," Dr. Stephenson said to the Morelli family. He then directed his attention to Brandon and winked.

"Keep the faith Brandon."

Brandon smiled, nodded, and said, "I will."

With that, the two men left and the door closed behind them.

The Morellis went back into the living room and sank back into the couches. It was very quiet for a couple of minutes as Brandon stared at his recovered treasure. His parents looked at each other and smiled knowing that their son was whole again. Finally his father broke the silence.

"Well," he said, "I'd say you're having a better than average weekend. Yesterday, you hit the game-winning home run, and today you got your lost compass back. Not bad kiddo."

"Yeah," Brandon replied, "it's so hard to believe, but all of it really happened. I just have one question."

"What's that sweetheart?" his mother asked.

"Are Grandma and Grandpa really coming, or was that part of the plan to disguise the surprise visit from Mr. C and Dr. Stephenson?"

Just then the doorbell rang.

"I think you're about to get your answer," Mr. Morelli said.

Once again Brandon ran to the door and opened it. Sure enough, his grandparents were standing there with big smiles on their faces.

"Grandma! Grandpa! You're here!"

"You bet we are!" his grandfather said.

"Let me look at you," his grandmother demanded. "Peter, will you look at how tall and how handsome our grandson is!"

Brandon looked back at his parents and smiled.

Chapter 34

LATER THAT EVENING, WHEN EVERYONE else in the house was asleep, Brandon was still awake in his dimly lit bedroom. He had brought the compass case into bed with him, and began to study its every detail as he held it gently in his hands. As he did so, he began to think about all that he and this object had been through. It had certainly been a whirlwind adventure! From the time he had first found the compass to the time it was returned to him by Mr. C, there was so much he had discovered about life. But the most important discovery Brandon made from this whole experience was the discovery of *self*. Brandon learned things about his character that he was never really aware of before. He learned that he had the ability to *trust* when he allowed Mr. Coviello to hold and study the compass case. He found that he had the power to *forgive* when his best friend, Shawn, betrayed him. He saw that he could resist *greed* when others were quick to give in to it. Finally, he learned that he had the ability to _heal_ after experiencing great pain when the compass was thought to be stolen. All of these things would give Brandon a greater sense of confidence and maturity as he approached his teenage years. Eventually he would realize what an important role the compass case played in all of this.

As he ran his thumb across the engraving of Columbus's signature, Brandon whispered a single word to himself.

"Faith."

Dr. Stephenson had told him that the compass would forever remain an object of faith. He would never know for sure if this old navigational instrument had ever touched the hands of the most famous explorer who ever lived. No one would. But that didn't matter to Brandon. Somehow, deep within himself, he knew.

As the years went by, Brandon Morelli kept his treasure a secret. He told no one about what Mr. Coviello had done to bring the compass back to him. It was too dangerous. However, he would always make time to visit his favorite teacher to talk about life, history, and sometimes the compass. The two of them would remain friends for years, and eventually, Mr. Coviello would be a mentor to Brandon as he became a teacher himself. "Feed the hungry minds" became Brandon's mission for the rest of his life.

Epilogue

Passage from a lost letter written by Christopher Columbus to his son Diego after Queen Isabella's death

"The soul of the Queen, our lady, has been brought to holy glory. Eternal God, our Lord, gives to all those who follow His path victory over things which appear impossible. Because her life was holy and prompt in the Lord's holy service, Spain obtained victory in attaining the knowledge and the wealth of the New World.

Her Highness was a woman of faith and generosity in a harsh and weary world. I will forever treasure her graciousness and the many blessings she bestowed on me.

I presently hold in my hand the token of admiration she gifted to me upon my return from the far seas, a beautifully crafted compass which bears the mark of the Admiral on its
case."

The End

About the Author

Brian Cannici is an elementary school teacher who has taken a special interest in children's literature. He is a graduate of Seton Hall University and Montclair State University, where he earned his Master of Education degree.

Mr. Cannici lives in New Jersey with his wife and two children.

Visit him at www.finding1492.com

Printed in the United States
112642LV00003B/329/P